Tales I Told My Mother

Robert Nye has the traditional storyteller's gifts for gripping narrative and spell-binding atmosphere. In this 'book in nine fictions' he takes us on a strange adventure of the imagination. By turns fantastic, grotesque, hilarious and terrifying, the stories, each entire on its own, build into each other like a jig-saw. Only as the characters grow taller and the themes deeper, as certain elements keep recurring like distorted echoes of what went before, do we realise that below the brilliant surface we are being invited to participate in mysteries that reflect a central mystery : the relationship of reality and imagination.

The nine tales range from the lyrical nostalgia of *Axel*, in which a young American regrets the simplicities of childhood, and in particular The Game he used to play with his father, to the slapstick comedy of *Mr Benjamin*, in which a racing tipster falls from his motorbike onto the lawn of a retired doctor—who keeps up his vocation by training flowers to grow crooked—and embarks on a long and absurdly perambulating monologue. A homosexual missionary with a taste for toasted mouse, a sea-captain who comes out in bruises when he listens to Schubert, the machinations of the Pre-Raphaelite 'mafia', and an enigmatic lady called Mary Murder, figure unforgettably in the others. While sometimes uproariously funny, this is not the book to read if you want to feel safe in your mind on a dark night. What it implies of the nature of truth and fiction is deeply disturbing, and the writing has an authentic cold sweat in it.

Tales I Told My Mother

ROBERT NYE

CALDER & BOYARS

LONDON

First published in Great Britain in 1969 by
Calder and Boyars Ltd
18 Brewer Street London W1

© 1969, Robert Nye

SBN 7145 0022 4 cloth edition
SBN 7145 0023 2 paper edition

Jacket reproduction of Rossetti's pen and indian ink
drawing *How They Met Themselves* by courtesy of
the Syndics of the Fitzwilliam Museum, Cambridge.

Printed in Great Britain by
Clarke, Doble & Brendon Ltd
Plymouth

TO AILEEN MY WIFE

CONTENTS

A Portuguese Person	11
Sdeath and Northangerland	29
Axel	33
Captain Rufus Coate	46
Howell	65
Mary Murder	78
The Wandering Jew	97
Mr Benjamin	107
The Amber Witch	141

The Pythagoreans said that the same things are repeated again and again. In this connection it is interesting to note the words of Eudemus, Aristotle's disciple (in the 3rd book of Physics). He says: Some people accept and some people deny that time repeats itself. Repetition is understood in different senses. One kind of repetition may be in the natural order of things (εἶδος), like repetition of summers and winters and other seasons, when a new one comes after another has disappeared; to this order of things belong the movements of the heavenly bodies and the phenomena produced by them, such as solstices and equinoxes, which are produced by the movement of the sun. But if we are to believe the Pythagoreans there is another kind of repetition. That means that I shall talk to you and sit exactly like this and I shall have in my hand the same stick, and everything will be the same as it is now and time, as it can be supposed, will be the same. Because if movements (of heavenly bodies) and many other things are the same, what occurred before and what will occur afterwards are also the same. This applies also to repetition, which is always the same. Everything is the same and therefore time is the same.

SIMPLICIUS, *Simplicii in Physicorum, IV, 12.*

For this goodly worke of which we are, and in which we live, hath not his being by Chaunce; on which opinion it is beyond mervaile by what chaunce any braine could stumble. For if it be eternall (as you would seeme to conceive of it) Eternity, & Chaunce are things unsufferable together. For that is chaunceable which happeneth; & if it happen, there was a time before it hapned, when it might not have happened; or els it did not happen; and so of chaunceable, not eternall, as now being, thē not being. And as absurd it is to thinke that if it had a beginning, his beginning was derived frō Chaunce: for Chaunce could never make all thinges of nothing: and if there were substaunces before, which by chaunce shoulde meete to make up this worke, thereon followes another bottomlesse pitt of absurdities. For then those substances must needes have bene from ever, and so eternall: and that eternall causes should bring forth chaunceable effects, is as sensible, as that the Sunne should be the author of darknesse.

PHILIP SIDNEY, *Arcadia, Lib. 3, Chap. 10.*

I have somewhere seen an anecdote of a sailor's mother, who believed all the strange lies which he told her for his amusement, but never could be persuaded to believe there could be in existence such a thing as a flying fish.

ROBERT SOUTHEY, *Madoc, Part 1, Book 5, Note.*

A Portuguese Person

CURRER POINTED at him and he began to die. The evening was cool. The wind smelt of smoke. Flame beckoned through the trees. A wrinkle of cloud shaped sometimes like a cross, sometimes like a snake or a worm, had formed out at the sea's rim and now warped over, letting fall thick warm drops the size of beans or nuts down upon them. A bee on a grey stone was stroking its wings with its legs. A footman strolled by, bald, yawning, leisurely, wearing a green coat with an otter collar, a tall fellow, slightly bent, with the depressed conceit of a consumptive, his face bleak and bony and slitlipped, mouth an uncouth droop, eyes redrimmed, the thin scar on his left cheek as white as a bleached fishbone, flexing his wrists deftly he blew his nose and looked in his handkerchief. The paths were strewn with ash. Tiny ripples flickered in the lake. Two young ladies had their heads together over Bradshaw on the green seat by the pagoda, one of them wore a velvet turban hat with grebe fur round it. A lark rehearsed its song, misleading, unappeasable. The waterwheel, weedslimed, hung dumb and dripping above its own broken image. A woman with a wicker basket on her arm walked about looking at the ground, slowly, as if bewildered, or lost, or going over her past life, her eyes bright with tears, her step complicated by anger, as though at the same time she was trying to protect an unhappiness she had elected to enjoy. A snail, tabernacle-backed, left hieroglyphics like crabbed lightning in its slow eccentric circuit of a root. Sunlight flashed on the brassy spectacles of a fiddler, his bow sawed and haggled at the strings, its horsehair was frayed, the instrument squealed, tobacco juice oozed

11

from the corners of his mouth like liquorice. A dog tore a frog to bits, worrying at it, the dog's teeth yellow, the frog's skin elastic and dewy, the dog biting and snapping and chewing and gnawing until the frog was no more than apple-peel.

Currer's finger was relentless. Ellis was afraid. The pupils of his eyes were milky. The hair on the back of his hands was red. The blood on the nettles looked like rust, it had gathered into sickly amber beads and some not trickled to the ground but hanging hard there to touch, a sweaty necklace.

Rosina's mind bled for hunger. She asked Currer why he always went in black. Black spelt strange constancy of heart, she said. Sometimes when he walked in the garden she had looked from her window and it had seemed to her that she saw a thick smoke walking there, a thick black smoke, though perhaps blue in the autumn air where it was soft beneath the trees. Black was the colour of unsatisfied desire. Black was the colour of the earth, and the earth would never be satisfied, not even when she had gone to bed to it.

She pinched tight her lips for scorn of pain.

The juniper bushes were brimming with birds.

Ellis's teeth chattered.

He groaned and moaned.

He was shivering in his throat.

His voice was slit.

Currer thrust a half-sovereign between his teeth.

Ellis spat it out.

No, he said, no.

The cloud went beyond the spur of the mountain. It drifted towards the gulf. It broke with being a cross and admitted a tall streak of evening sky which the sun wondered upon, so that Currer could almost believe Rosina when she said that it was a burning bridge, and asked him if he could not see the fine folk who danced upon it. Up and down, she said, round and about, to sweet music, their arms linked, woman and man. Love makes them dance, said she, and my heart dances to that tune.

12

But Currer was newly come from the burial of the dead, and he did not believe her. The dead lay where the linden stained the wall. Pleasing, thought Currer, to lie under linden, never to lose shadow even when the summer sun towered, to lie quite quiet and still and naked in the cool earth, the dark earth, the lean convenient earth, to forget, never again to have the heart pull you back from the night, from going into the night, from taking to yourself an honest night, to lie quite still and quiet and forget the heart. He had put them to earth. They were well there.

Currer found that he could span with his fingers the spots where the blood had gathered.

A stalk-legged bird perched upon the waterwheel.

Acton hurried down the dark oak stair. The curtains were thick and heavy, sunlight found fault with the entwined fruit and flowers designed in worsted on them, there was a monstrous panelled mantelpiece reaching from the floor to the ceiling, its intricate fretwork of compartments was filled with silverplated candlesticks, brass dishes hammered into complicated ornamental relief from the reverse side, blue china vases crammed with peacock feathers, skullsize pieces of amber, tins of cocoa, crucifixes, and a Bryant and May's matchbox.

Rosina trembled as Acton bound her hand and foot. Then he took from his pocket an old cloth, filthy, stinking of fish, still stuck all over with bright scales, and would have tied it about her staring amberflecked eyes, but Currer saw and snatched off his silk neckerchief, praying the Duke would use this instead. Which Acton did, with a curt bow to mock them. And then the thumbscrews were fastened on Rosina, and she was asked again kindly to confess. But she only shook her blinded head, her hair tumbling forth over the rack. She was naked save for the Limerick shawl.

Ellis's eyes had the look of a woman who gazes down the blue uncertain shaft of a well at noon, her elbows on the curb, her highcheeked face in her hands.

The hair on the back of his hands was red, the Judas colour

13

of the houses burning. He was a wild guest. His boots were bloody, streaked with blood amid the dust and mud, sleek black thighboots veined with blood.

A worm ate at Rosina's heart.

Pity put tears in Currer's tongue. He said to Ellis, I love you.

The bitterness was sealed up in the flowers.

What colour should a priest of God wear then, if not His decent black? Currer asked Rosina.

She sighed. I speak not of priests, but of the man my father, she said.

Currer felt as if she had not spoken a word to him but had thrown a handful of leaves into his eyes. His spirit cracked. He put his fingers together to pray, but his hands seemed only for letting go.

Ellis was three parts dead. His flesh was stained, it crumbled. His arms withered, they folded like a golliwog's. His cheeks fell in. Currer could see the bad bones through the side of his face, already swart green with the phosphorescence which plays about the remains of a saint, or rotting fish. This lustre, Currer noticed, soon dissipated itself—he supposed, as the blood ran cold and stiffened the veins of the heart.

Currer was but little surprised to find Ellis subject to death. Ellis was meat, after all, like the rest of them, a mere mess of gristle and ligaments and humours, a piece of sublunar anatomy, a bladder with two mouths, two doors, his stomach sustained no doubt by a soft kell or caul, as was usual in the creatures.

Ellis's clothes, also, were too big for him now that he was dying. He wore a kind of frockcoat, fashioned from brown leather, embroidered with braid. This coat, buttoned and girdled, began to look several sizes too large, hanging loosely from his broken shoulders.

His face went yellow, then white, then the colour of putrefaction, it had a mildewy fur on it, like a sort of sour spermatical porridge.

14

Pale juice ran from his nostrils.

One of his cheekbones penetrated the liquescent flesh with a soft plop, it was grained with that blowzy brickcoloured substance known as ruddle, giving him a rouged guise, precious, perverse, coquettish.

Ellis's eyes had fallen open and he was staring fixedly at a point in nothing.

His legs tried to walk even as he was dead, but his corpse toppled over and was still, a parcel of moist nerves on the cobbles.

Currer looked down at him. He said, I love even your smell now that you are dead.

For the body had begun to stink, it was true, and a bluefly worried briefly at the pane.

But there was no window.

No window, and no house, and no dark oak stair, and no threshold with streaks of light flung here and there through the torn hinges.

In truth Currer was standing in a pleasure ground and there was green grass growing between the stones.

There was a grotto, a quaint castellated building in poured concrete, of irregular hexagonal form, studded with shells and stones and crystals, jagged, dramatic, cantilevered, allowing two apartments open to the gardens.

There was a temple, a circular domed colonnade, gentle, subtle, a cocoon of spun glass achieved by a double row of soaring pillars and pilasters.

There was a window, blond with sunlight, where one watched Currer, her ring against the glass making a queenly sound.

Currer was standing in a pleasure ground, then, and his daughter Rosina must have been perhaps twelve years old, yes, in her twelfth year, a witty child, her veins like wine, her paps like honey, her thighs like a triumphal arch, unfortunately sapphic, but able to speak the Latin tongue. That pleasant priest was taking a walk with her, there in the Spani-

15

ards, showing her the proud insectivorous plants, and the pea-
cocks overflowingly restless, and the unseizable butterflies, and
the statues. He had been explaining to her that the most
immaculate contraceptive known to man is the simple water-
lily, when, in turning about a glossy-leaved shrub, possibly an
azalea, though he feared in pestering reality it might more
nicely have been a humble rhododendron, they saw their lord
the Duke standing on a brief hummock of ground, clad in a
cloak of dim silk, and engaged in sullen dispute with a fellow
in green who, from his towering inchoate gestures, Currer
took to be of noble birth yet the Duke's inferior. Father and
daughter turned back modestly into the fragrant shade, and
stood there listening, hand in hand.

For his own part, Acton was saying, if he was to be allowed
to have one, he could not believe that Ellis was dead. A caustic
voluptuous death like that made almost a sexual process of
dying. Or should they say, rather, that it was a fatal hap-
pening? a piece of politics? an accident? even, heartfailure?
the articles of Ellis's extinction all signed long ago in some
cool blue room where the doctors pointed with ferules to a
lighted chart, tracing the journey of the natural poison
through his frame, showing him the probable growth of his
death within him, the putative shape of his corpse, the final
skeleton being father to the man, saying, Here, yes, and, Here,
soon, unamazedly, properly, with discreet professional appre-
ciation, the sympathy being the business of another doctor,
this one a doctor with a scored teak desk and eyebrows and a list
of words on the blotter before him, a thesaurus of grief, terms
of pity and comfort under separate headings : *Believes in God,
Doesn't*. It would indeed be pleasant to suppose that Ellis had
suffered from some slow wasting sickness that was subtly quick-
ened—who knew how?—by Currer's idle pointing at him.
Certainly Currer had not meant to kill him. Currer would not
hurt a fly, everyone knew that. If his wife had been alive—
16

Acton asked the green fellow to forgive him for calling that woman his wife, but he had forgotten her name—she would have confirmed this. As it was, the green fellow could ask his Worship. Even though his Worship was a high darkhearted man, scoffing at the holy gospel and the preaching of the Word, and openly and without shame making mock of the servants of God, he would tell him. Aye, said Acton, even though his Worship sat cold there in the castle behind walls thick enough to put a man in, nursing his rainbow snout by the fire, picking at his boils and listening to that brainwormed Bastard, his son, banging doomsday on the drum he bore about with him everywhere, his Worship, his Hugeness, his Guts, the Nothing of Nothing, greased cruel potbelly whoremaster, got fat from bloodsucking, his Pittilessness, the Bully of Tosspotdom, his Crapulousness, his Concupiscence, his Hoggish Highness, his Infernal Indifference. Let the green fellow ask even his Worship. He would tell him: Currer? He's a real softy! A jellyfish! A little epitome of the leavings of nature's workshop! A compound of all sorts and sexes! A wheyfaced hermaphrodite!

A sexual process of death, Acton went on. Yes, that was true. That was about the measure of the truth of it. There had been some gory almost orgiastic thing in the way Ellis responded to Currer's words. Such power in speech? Acton wondered. Not even he could believe it. And for the opposite— or what Acton presumed to be the opposite—of what could be contained in the words to work such fatal alteration in Ellis? If the beloved died, always and always, whenever the lover spoke his love, what then? Acton demanded. The world was not so inward, so withdrawn, so warmly to be harmed. No. It could not afford to be. Currer had not killed him. All Acton could think was that Ellis had already been ill, grievously sick, diseased, near death, and Currer's abrupt declaration from the shadows had frightened him in some way with its passion, its threat of care, and made him give up the ghost.

Lies, Acton said thoughtfully, more to himself than to the fellow in green. When he looked at it honestly he had to admit that Currer had enjoyed Ellis's dying. Even as he was saying he loved him he knew he was killing him. Yes, Currer had murdered Ellis all right. He had twisted his heart in his fingers and wrung it out and picked it to twitters while Ellis, the poor fool, just stood there with his sawney mouth open and the sawney light shining on his sawney spectacles. Currer had known his finger was killing him, too. Of course he had. Which was not to say that Acton knew how Currer had done it. As a matter of fact, he didn't. He didn't have a manual of perfect murder to offer the green fellow. Simply, from the moment when Currer stepped forth to where the sun worshipped the jetty cups, and became aware—conscious, if the green man liked—of how deep and furious was his love for Ellis, he had been able to flex his finger in his sleeve and take joy in its crisp crackling as he did so, knowing that at any time he chose he could point at Ellis and make him change for better or for worse, indicate the corpse in him, if need be, unloose that angel. Acton knew, that is, the power of Currer's feeling there in him, and knew that he had both wanted and not-wanted to exercise it—rather, to use it. (One did not exercise love, Acton supposed.) Even now Currer did not find it all used up.

The green fellow looked nervous. Acton barely acknowledged him. Currer could kill again by pointing, he said. He was sure of it. Fortunately Currer no longer felt he loved anyone enough to want to single them out for that sort of attention, that kind of barbarous blessing. How to explain Ellis's murder then . . . for murder it was. Had Currer put the finger on him to enjoy his power? to demonstrate the depth and direction of his love, love, all love? to point him the way to death? Currer had loved Ellis. Yes. And Ellis was better off dead. Yes. That was true. But in his heart of hearts Acton knew that Currer had not killed Ellis for any reasons of well-wishing, of benevolence, no, nor out of emotional discretion,

18

an economy of amends. No. Currer had killed Ellis because he had pointed at him and Currer's finger killed. To go beyond that statement was to go too far. But how could Acton ever rest content this side of 'too far'?

The green fellow flourishing with his hands but offering no answer to Acton's question, the two of them strolled off in the direction of the mineral springs.

Currer and Rosina went to stand in the place where the high ones had been standing. It pleased Currer to have his shadow fall where the Duke's had lately been, to think of himself as Duke, and the Duke as nobody, a humblebumble drone of the Word, a parish thing.

As he stood thus, in vain amaze, dreaming a cloak of dimmest silk about him to fondle and fold his hands in softly while he rebuked his henchmen, Rosina of a sudden cried, Look.

She had seen a ring lying on the turf. She picked it up. It was a gimmal ring, consisting of three gold links, turning upon a sly pivot, which when pressed clicked shut in a solid circle, representing eternity, a solid yet impermanent circle, representing eternity. A diminutive outstretched hand was affixed to the side of each of the exterior links. When the ring was shut these two babyish hands clasped and fitted into each other, enclosing a heart attached to the central link, which was minutely notched to make the grip the faster.

Currer explained to his daughter that such rings were once popular, although he did not approve of the custom or its popularity. She asked him what the custom was and he told her that it was to break the ring asunder at the time of betrothal, the man keeping the upper link, the woman the lower, and the priest the middle one. When the marriage compact was performed at the altar, the three members of the ring were again united, and the ring used in the ceremony.

Rosina pointed out to her father that there was a posy

inscribed within the hoop of the ring, which became apparent only when the triple band was set tight, and the posy said, *And this also shall pass away.*

The sun sinking at his back, Currer turned and said to Rosina, Come, daughter, let us haste after our lords, and when we reach them do you say, Serenissimi principes quis vestrum hunc annulum deperditit? and if one should answer, Ego, then give the gimmal ring to him.

Rosina agreed to do this bidding, but in going forward she trembled and blushed and snatched at her goffered flounces and boisterous foamy farthingale and came ascamper back to her father, unable.

Currer exhorted her more strongly to the errand, and promised her a pink silk fan with Valenciennes lace, two green cocks' feathers, a gilt metal waist belt, Genoese buttons, and a gold wirework butterfly for her hair, if she would.

Coming then down the chequered walk between clipped trees towards the springs, Currer halted and whispered to Rosina, Courage, for Acton and the green man paced only a few steps before them and already wended themselves towards the jetty cups.

Rosina ran, but swerved and stopped and span about again, because she became affrighted at the spurs of the two lordly ones, which rattled and wrangled monstrously as they walked on the cobbles veined between with green.

Howbeit the Duchess saw all this hesitant adventure of Currer's daughter's from the open window of the grotto, where she lay bare-breasted to take the sun in the upper apartment, and she called to her husband, There is a strange girl behind you, my pet, and she would speak with you, as it seems. Look, is she not beautiful?

Acton turned on his spurred heel and he smiled when he saw Rosina's hair with the sun in it, so that her courage came quick back to her tongue, and her wit also, and holding up

20

the gimmal ring in her pretty dainty fingers like minnows she said, in Latin, all that her father had bidden her say.

The gentlemen both marvelled at her speech, and Acton, feeling on his finger, answered, Dulcissima puella ego perdidi.

Rosina reached him the ring.

For this he stroked her cheeks as smooth as the good crust on new bread and asked, Sed quaenam es et unde venis?

Rosina answered not a word, but pointed with her eyes towards Currer where he lurked some meek way off.

The Duke muttered to the green fellow and beckoned Currer to come near. That done, he considered Currer's person as though he had painted him and was now disagreeably surprised by the evidence his own talents.

Who are you? he asked.

Stunned by the illdeserved brutality of the question, Currer set himself to finding an answer to it, and began the story of his heart.

The next thing that good priest knew the Duke lay dead on the cobbles, his crooked fingers twined in the few unkempt grasses that grew between. Why did Currer point? Did he want to kill him? He does not think so, no. He does not think he knew he had any comfortable strength in his love to kill the Duke. It is true, of course, that he kept still and quiet as he observed Acton about to die, but then that was a matter of courtesy, of good manners. He supposes that he could have foregone or superseded punctilios for the occasion. He supposes that he should have stopped, or pointed at the sun like Galileo Galilei. He supposes that he might have saved the Duke. But will you believe Currer when he says that it never occurred to him to do so?

Well, we will not worry overmuch about belief. There are no problems of belief, only of faith. Let us say that he will agree, Currer, for the time being, to believe in you, gentle reader, purely to save himself from the more obvious errors of

21

selflove that might arise, irascible ghosts, if he indulged in argument with himself. You may believe or disbelieve as his story pleases you. Let us try to have the telling pure, without too much story, then the story will fill it. The storying, that is the point.

When they saw that the Duke was dead they grew angry. They said that Currer had killed him, that he had been his enemy, that Currer was a truant, a Jacobite, a traitor. They alleged that his father had been master of an unsuccessful horsetramway, and that his failure had embittered Currer's spirit. They claimed that Currer had murdered Acton because he hated him. In vain did Currer protest that he had loved him. No, they said, you are a supernatural cut-throat, a killer. You must in turn be killed. By whose orders? Currer asked. By the Queen's, they said. And they showed him a ring then that they said was hers. Currer did not know whether it was or it was not, to be honest. He dares say it could have been hers, genuinely. It was blue sapphire, and it sweated when Currer touched it to his lips. Here, they cried, don't let him do that, the bloody Cromwell, he'll be putting some spit on the Queen's ring next and then where shall we be. They took the ring away from him and put it in a black bag. Currer does not think he saw it again. What are you going to do with my daughter? he said. He was nervous on her behalf. Daughter? they said. They were sneering. You have no daughter. Currer looked about for Rosina but she was gone. He comforted himself with the thought that she might have slipped away into one of the groves, or the grotto, or the pagoda, or perhaps the maze. He lit a cigar and pretended to admire the evening. He rather wished he was a hundred miles away.

Polpo is coming, one of them said. A crowd had gathered about the pool fed by the chalybeate fountain, still sustaining bright heartless egress from the throat of the strangled swan. This crowd consisted, so far as Currer could judge, of

22

the sort of persons one might expect to find in the Spaniards at that time of day. That is, Smithfield butchers, the knackers of Turnmill Street, and the less respectable denizens of Field Lane. The man who had said that Polpo was coming was a cut above the sweaty mediocrity of the rest. He was a lean man, with a dark face and a hook nose, a Portuguese, in Currer's reckoning. Not a native of that country, Currer thought, but bearing an air of it with him. A monocle dangled on his chest, making a little anxious dot of light. His eyes were small and dull and he held Currer's sleeve as he talked, not to restrain him but as if to study the texture of the cloth between his thumb and forefinger, yet, all the same, there was a feeling that if he wanted to, if he needed to, if he chose to, he could easily restrain him. He knew this feeling and Currer knew it, and there was this not unpleasant bond of unease between them. Currer asked the Portuguese who Polpo was and he shrugged. Currer grew scorchingly angry at this shrug. What right have you to treat me thus? he cried, and was surprised to find that his voice laughed with hysteria. Where is my daughter? he went on. You must have seen her. She is beautiful, twelve years old, with caliper splints on her left leg, her name is Rosina. Where is she? Let me go. I have done nothing. I am innocent. The Portuguese smiled. Citizen, he said, you shake your head like a horse. I don't say that you are guilty, mind. That's not for you or me to decide, is it? We're not expected to judge each other, after all, that's in the law. You are neither a fool nor perfect, but you are assuredly the dupe of your own greenness. And that makes you an ignoramus—because you're content to go on in it and on. Well, Polpo will inform you, that he will! When the Portuguese had finished saying this Currer asked him if he had finished, politely, and the Portuguese said he had—or, rather, inclined his long head graciously that it was so—and Currer offered him a cigar from the straining band of them he carried in his cap. Currer's fingers were still shaking with temper, but he doubts if the Portuguese noticed this. The Portuguese refused the cigar with pleasure, saying that he did not dare smoke one because his heart was weak. Currer's anger was gone in a wink, and he felt an intemperate tenderness for the Portuguese instead, considering his person thoughtfully and sucking on the cigar. He was a man of below average stature, but broadshouldered, his hair was black and somewhat lank, with sideboards that delved almost into his collar, lending him a disturbingly Victorian aspect, indeed, now Currer comes to think of it, he will tell you directly that the words which came into his head at this moment of close looking at the stranger were : Matthew Arnold. His lips were thin, pursed, shrewdly cruel, his eyebrows were bushy and held in a sarcastic position of enquiry, he had no scars or boils or other distinguishing marks. It was the face of a ghost crippled by confidence. Currer noticed that he was wearing false eyelashes, one of them hung askew and dangling from its lid, like a wounded moth. As Currer looked at it he seemed to see the Portuguese limp away into his own small eyes, which were dull blue in colour and, Currer fancies, shortsighted. When Currer says limped he does not mean that the Portuguese would have limped in the normal course of things, like his poor Rosina. The Portuguese was a man to affect a limp out of positiveness, out of his own sentimental expectation of himself, is what Currer means. He wore a faded chalky denim jacket of the sort that housepainters sometimes have, or truckdrivers in what Currer supposes to be American films. His shoes, Currer noticed with approval, were old but eagerly polished, catching the last light of the sun through the avenue of larches whispering west of where they stood. Even as Currer searched the face and person of the Portuguese for some clue as to his real reason for accosting him, he saw that the other man was absurdly interested in the sunset, not in the least put out by his unwavering regard, and he was touched by this. Currer turned and looked where he looked. The sun was posted at the end of the avenue above a white fountain that appeared black in the distance and what with the gloom of the avenue.

24

It hung above the dark fountain like a ball bouncing on a jet of wine, only this was a ball not at the mercy of the fountain, nor the indifferent air, but placed in the evening here for objects to dispose themselves about, to find pattern and meaning in having association with it, attendance upon it, being parts of the picture the sun was burning centre of. Do you know, said Currer's companion, that sentence in Coleridge which goes something like this: In dreams I do not recollect that state of feeling common when awake, of thinking on one subject and looking at another. Before Currer had time to answer as he would have wished there was heard a baying of hounds afar off, and then the sharp thin sound of a horn imperfectly blown, and the artisans—who had been standing listless and superstitious about the Duke's corpse on the stones of the courtyard, some praying, some gossiping, some bargaining, some just walking up and down and kicking at each other's heels—began to huddle together. Currer sensed an ignoble excitement spreading amongst them and heard a whispered, He is coming, Polpo is coming, Polpo. Currer looked then at the Portuguese but he was engrossed in knotting his tie in a new knot and gave every appearance of having no further care if Currer lived or died. For himself, Currer was persuaded that it was death herself coming towards him somewhere through the pleasure ground, though the unfairness of it brought tears to his eyes and he would have been glad of the chance to justify himself to someone. None of the crowd looked interested in Currer or his fate, however. They had begun to talk amongst themselves, so low and fast that he could not isolate any of the words they uttered. From the odd cadence of the conversations, though, Currer gained a quaint but definite impression that they were talking in a foreign language, Dutch perhaps, or Croat, or Welsh. He thought he caught the word Polpo once, accompanied by an ear-munching grin and a chopping motion with the hand held out stiff at waist height, very quick and brutish, which sent a shiver down his spine. But it would be wrong to say that Currer was

25

frightened. He was, permit a certain accuracy, in a state of profound and outreaching apprehensiveness, and felt some haphazard tugging at the nerve strings. His chief anxiety, in scanning the blank faces that made up the crowd, was to find someone to whom he might communicate his hesitations, his suspicions, his confessions, his shyness even, before the coming of this fell Polpo. Yes, shyness. Currer will admit it. He was blushing. If the Portuguese noticed that Currer's cheeks were red he said nothing, nor gave any sign of it. He was suddenly the familar wellwisher, urbane and careless, and looked at Currer as if he were a train about to leave a station, an express train with a wedding party on board, the luggage packed, the bride unknown to him. He had knotted his tie to his fingers' satisfaction and stood patting it for, Currer supposed, his approval also. Currer thinks that kind of knot is called a Windsor knot, but he is not adept at the knotting of ties so he could not swear to it, besides he has noticed how the knot one draws at one's own neck always feels and looks unlike the same knot at someone else's neck. This fellow's tie was green, woollen, knitted. Currer dislikes green woollen ties. The fact of the tie being of a sort Currer particularly dislikes, abominates even, and for good reasons, made the Portuguese's new rôle of selfelected impartial wellwisher the harder to stomach, especially as Currer wanted to tell him of his shyness before Polpo. The baying of the hounds was nearer now. Currer pictured them at full pent through the car-park. The Portuguese was shifting from foot to foot, surrounded by himself, scuffing at the cobbles with his shiny brown shoes. He seemed, to Currer's eyes, ill, tainted, sallow, certainly sick with a crude impatience to get him gone. The idea crossed Currer's mind that the Portuguese was jealous of the air he took in breathing. He wanted not more air, but Currer's air. He wanted Currer's lungs suitably collapsed and out of the way. Also, there was something implacably *military* about the fellow. Currer wanted to salute him, corrected the want immediately, and said, What will Polpo do with me? The Portu-

26

guese shrugged. The usual, he said. How that shrug annoyed Currer! But he kept a civil tongue. What is the usual? he said. The Portuguese grinned. Currer saw the stones under the waters of his eyes. The man was considering him as an undertaker might, measuring trade. He will masturbate you, he said. Then Currer laughed out loud in the idiot's face. No kidding? he said. No kidding, said the Portuguese. The baying of hounds seemed just beyond the clump of trees to their right. But he can't do that, Currer said. Why not? asked the Portuguese. Because I'm not queer, Currer said. I don't want him to. I don't want that. You're joking. I'm not queer and have never been queer. It's the one socalled vice . . . The long sallow face of the Portuguese (was it a trick of the failing light that made his forehead seem sprinkled with blackheads?) sneered at Currer and mimicked his voice. Socalled vice, he said. A silly smile was smeared across his face. We must look, it occurred to Currer, like a duel. Then Polpo came out of the trees. Currer was disappointed. Polpo was an absolute insignificance. Currer cannot remember anything of how Polpo looked, probably for this reason—that he looked much like anyone one does not look at. The only uncommon thing about him was his voice. Currer realised at once that there were no hounds. Polpo's hounds were himself. He made a noise in his throat as he came like the brisk baying of thirsty dogs. Currer wondered where he had read of disease like that. Was it not a species of lycanthropia, which Avicenna calls cucubuth, others lupinam insaniam, or wolf-madness? Was it not Glatisant, the Questing Beast, in Malory, that made a noise like the baying of parched hounds? Whether or not it was in Malory, or Currer only dreamed he read of it there, he will leave for you to look up because he's damned if he's going to run the risk of tempting whatever-it-is with certainties. Perhaps it is not in Malory but Chrétien de Troyes. Perhaps it is not Glatisant but Dormarth. Goodbye now, said the Portuguese. He did not move. But the sunlight was walking away from him. Wait, Currer said, won't you wait and discuss that beautiful Coleridge which . . . But the Portuguese was gone, and the crowd was gone. And when Currer looked down where the jetty cup had tumbled, he saw that they had dragged the Duke's corpse with them. Only his cloak remained there, like a silky puckered puddle, Acton's dim cloak. There was only Currer and Polpo. I am kindness itself, said Polpo. You understand? he said. I wish you well. I will always wish you well. He had a box sticking out of his pocket. He took out the box. It was handsome, antique, ebony, a family heirloom perhaps? Out of the handsome box he took a razor. It was what is called a cut-throat razor. That is to say, it was an open razor of the kind that is used in barbers' shops. He unfolded the razor with a wary caress. What are you going to do? Currer asked, as calmly as he could. Masturbate you, said Polpo. But I don't understand, Currer said. I am kindness itself, said Polpo. There must have been some, Currer said. The milk of human kindness, said Polpo. But the razor, Currer said. The razor also is kind, said Polpo. When he had done Currer remembers nothing until he heard the sly mocking bird-voice of the Portuguese, as it were a long way off, explaining something to the crowd. He thought I did not know he blushed, he was saying. Good old De Castro, one called out, and the cry was taken up: Good old De Castro, good old De Castro. Someone laughed. It was a young girl's laugh. It was Rosina. Currer's daughter. Yes, his heart leapt. He heard the clink of her calipers on the cobbles veined between. But it was the green fellow, plainly inferior, who delivered his official eulogy. Shame, he said shrilly, shame. Look, added the Portuguese, by way of epitaph: he's blushing elsewhere now.

The Story of Sdeath and Northangerland
from the Eighth Book of the
History of the Kingdom of Angria
by Patrick Branwell Brontë

SDEATH BEAT his wife and this was bad luck because she was Northangerland's sister. Northangerland had been Sdeath's best friend. Quite likely there was some dab or streak or dribble of uranism to their fellowship, for no sooner had Sdeath married Northangerland's sister than he began hanging her up by the heels and chastising her devoutly with a thin cane. In return, she gave her husband a copy of Elizabeth Barrett Browning's SONNETS FROM THE PORTUGUESE[1], also a ring inscribed with the posy, *Wear me out, Love shall not waste.*

Northangerland went so far as to marry Sdeath's sister, who had anal catarrh and was a misery besides, just on purpose not to beat her and so prove that one could be an Angrian and a married pacifist without losing honour, but Sdeath took no note at all. Every night it was the thin cane (which he kept soaking in a vat of Bannerman's pure malt vinegar for the response) and up on the golden hook with her and down with her drawers, etcetera.

Northangerland bit his thumbs. He did not much like his sister, but he liked Sdeath's sister even less, especially now he was married to her and could not beat her (for the ignored example). Then his own sister died, possibly on account of Sdeath's attentions, and Northangerland decided that he

---

[1] As Branwell died in 1848 and Mrs Browning's wreath of sonnets was not published until 1850, it is probable that this is one of Charlotte's pieces of embroidery.

adored the memory of her. His life found music in hatred of Sdeath, the cruel brother-in-law.

As an outward sign of his inner resolve, Northangerland began to consort with his cousin, the Lady Augusta Geraldine Almeda, otherwise known as A. G. A., who lived by bread alone in a house called Withering, and who was the sworn enemy of Sdeath. Sdeath, for his part, plotted deliciously to kill Northangerland, snapping rooks and bishops in his passion.

Now A. G. A. was a toxophilite humanist, well able, as Shakespeare says, to clap in the clout at twelve score, and carry a forehand shaft a fourteen and a fourteen and a half. She enjoyed the company of three bows, the first made of wych, the second made of ash, and the principal of yew. Each of these instruments was a foot taller than herself. Her arrows, winged with grey goose feathers, were made of fustic, sallow, turkeywood, and hornbeam. She loved nothing better than a shooting match, and one day arranged such a match with her crony and cousin, the bold Northangerland.

On the morning of the day appointed for the shooting match, Northangerland rode forth to the field with his wife and admirers. His wife, alas, developed Allegory and turned back before they had gone half way. As she was riding home again she met her brother, his eyes full of bruises. Smelling mischief, she snatched hold of the tail of his horse. Sdeath flicked an unobtrusive peg behind the horse's left ear, and the creature shat voluminously. Still Mrs Northangerland hung on. So Sdeath drew his short sword and cut off her arm at the elbow. Not to be discomfited, she threw a hawk at his head with her hand that was left. Sdeath dodged like a green-grocer, and bolted.

This was his arrangement for the murder of Northangerland: Northangerland was to be engaged in argument as to the nature of the scepticism of Joseph Glanvill, and whether indeed it was sufficient to merit his being considered a true disciple of Pyrrho of Elis, and then when the melée was at the full a man called Mann was to trot up and drop a tortoise on the victim's head—Northangerland, like Aeschylus, being bald. Still and all, Sdeath remarked to the assassin, watch out for Northangerland's Cornish catamite, Iago Ink, the merest marasmic atomy of a mortal, a shrimp, a grub, a monad, less than nothing is, but I tell you that homunculus has the Devil in his fingernail.

Trust me, said Mann, spitting without fuss.

But when they came up to Northangerland's people and began, Iago Ink caught the assassin by the ankle before he had a chance to get the tortoise out of his satchel, trepanned him, and dipped his hands to flick and wash them in Mann's brains, all with a chaste smile of *taedium vitae*.

Sdeath withdrew, vexed.

He tried a subtler tack. He sent a woman, her name was Mother Clap, to knock on the door of a certain parson, astrologer to Northangerland, whose character is contained in one sentence : He was too good to be bored by God. Mother Clap soon made herself at home in the astrologer's house. She played his clavichord and spoke of backsliding. He made her a refreshing dish of gunpowder tea.

That night, in the dead of the dark, Mother Clap leaped out of bed and accused the astrologer of sexual congress in the Italian style. He denied it. He had been bathing, he said, and was moved to irritability by the grains of sand which had insinuated themselves between the crisp sheets. Mother Clap persisting in her charge, the astrologer fled.

In the morning, Mother Clap went home and told her sons, Nick, Scratch, and Horny, of her adventures.

Ram him, said Nick.

Jam him, said Scratch.

And with a forty horsepower damn him, said Horny.

The three lads went out and murdered the astrologer in the reading room of the public library.

Distraught by the prospect of Northangerland's vengeance, the sons of Mother Clap sought sanctuary in a nunnery. They were received.

When Northangerland discovered where the lads were hiding, he and two of his men dressed in nun's weeds and presented themselves before the abbess, claiming to be emissaries from Lesbos. They were welcomed.

To cut a short story shorter, Northangerland and his assistants succeeded in awakening the interest of Nick and Scratch and had recourse to the razor in protecting their virtue. Soon two Clap heads slept apart from their bodies.

But what of Horny? Horny was suspicious of the intruders' hips, and not to be tempted. Besides, he was busy enough, being stout and cordial, and hence in demand among the younger nuns, for mortification of the fleshy part.

At length, however, one of Northangerland's lieutenants drew Horny into the sport of hanging him. The lieutenant sacrificed his life. Northangerland throttled Horny with his own whip.

Their work done, the surviving pseudonuns sprang to the saddle, kilted up their skirts, and rode singing into a dawn that was all blood and foxy.

Seven years later, Northangerland died of burns after his wife had dashed a ladleful of scalding mead into his eyes. Whether she did this deliberately, or was clumsy in her one-armed condition, is not known. When the news of his enemy's end was brought to Sdeath he could not stop laughing, choked, and was launched on a chickenbone into eternity.

Mrs Northangerland inherited both estates, but gave all to the poor, and set up house at Withering with A. G. A. She had by the end a local name for one-arm archery, drawing the bow between her teeth.

Axel

SHE WAS a warm unwondering woman, Axel's mother, warm yet somehow, by some trick her son never got the hang of, distant amid the warmth, as if she beckoned always beyond the arm's reach so that Axel blamed his arm, cursed it even, where truly it was his mother who should have been cursed for her habit of being, as it were, in love elsewhere.

When Axel thinks of his mother he thinks of a garden where they used to go together when he was a child. Possibly he used to sail a paper boat in the pool in this garden, but that would more likely be a retrospective invention of his imagination, or something he read in a book of someone else's childhood that has impinged on his memory of his childhood. Axel's was not really a paper boat childhood. He is not Shelley. Even had he wished to be Shelley . . . ? Whether such gloomy romantic accretions are valid he cannot say. He prefers to persuade himself that there is a certain art, a bright art of necessity, in stripping them away, in having the thing clean, the memory small and exact, dull even, and selfdiscrediting, but perfect.

This garden formed part of a priory. It could not have been far outside the city, for Axel seems to remember that they were driven there regularly, on Sunday afternoons perhaps. There were grey walls, scribbled over with moss, that were warm to the hand even quite late in autumn, so closely they held the least last bit of sun. Also there were paths of white pebbles that wound in and out of the flowerbeds. Do not ask Axel the names of the flowers in that garden. He has never had the smallest interest in flowers or birds or mysteries of that sort. He remembers only the pools. He wants to tell you something about the pools. The pools and the statues and the gargoyles above the drinkingbowls that were here and there in the walls. Mostly, the pools.

Were there *fish* in those pools? Who knows. Definitely there were *thoughts*. The nuns used to walk there sometimes, in winter Axel reckons, arm in arm, their veils and robes as involuted as cabbages, nuns, walking cabbages.

But do not think Axel is irreligious, an atheist, a Protestant, anything of that sort. He merely tells you how it is in his memory of this garden. When he is asked, as he has been, to fill in one of the forms which demand of us that we declare our faith, he never has any difficulty in making himself clear : *Heretic.*

Axel's mother used to stand for hours just gazing into those pools in the priory garden. She rarely stooped to dip her long white fingers in their coolness, nor let her shadow fall across the carpet of lilypads, nor consulted her image there, no. Axel's mother was not vulgar of her beauty. She liked just to stand still at the water's unruffled edge and think what there was to be thought.

The nuns grew used to her standing there. Did they ever smile at her, or speak to Axel? Or smile at Axel, or speak to her? Axel thinks not.

If it is true that nuns walked in the garden, and Axel can almost swear they did, for they are there in his head, nuns, white nuns, possibly Ursulines or nuns of the Visitation, and his mother in the blue dress, always in the blue dress, with the pale blue parasol folded in her hand like a question, or furled, yes, furled rather, the pale blue parasol furled in her hand like a question, in its crotchet cover, leaves and flowers connected by bars, jasmine pattern, and the bright shoes with the buckles, standing by the side of one of the little round pools, litanies in her look, and the sun sinking lower and lower, until it sits

34

on top of the moss-encrusted wall, squats gold astride the moul-
dering mossy wall, above the begonias, what a lie, above those
flowers without petals that grew there, and Axel stroll-
ing about the paths, the paths of white pebbles, taking
care never to kick the white pebbles, or otherwise dis-
turb them, taking care *never* to run, or hop, or dance,
for this is a priory garden, this is not a pleasure ground, this
is a holy place, and they are fortunate to be allowed within it,
behaving himself, conducting himself with composure, walking round and round, looking, just looking, blind to the flowers
and the birds, Axel even seems to think that birds rarely came
within the garden, doing nothing that he now can put a name
to, touching the walls perhaps, feeling the old stone grow cold
as the sun first hardens and then goes off it, climbing down
and walking away west, stained green where it has been sitting,
leaving only shadow, grey shadow, chalk shadow, mauve, then
softer blue shadow, a sour winepress, big drops, and then black
shadow and the wall abruptly chill and the little ridges in it
sharper and newly hurtful under his palms and fingertips, and
the garden empty when Axel looks up, empty and filled with
dusk, and the smell of smoke on the air, and the nuns all
gone that had walked there, two by two, in crisp tormented
white in the sun, the nuns gone and the sun gone, and the
garden old and cold and empty save for where his mother
stands, quite still, so still, so constantly, so irresolutely, so fleet-
ingly still, *you would have thought she was a visitor from
somewhere else*, a revenant, a fugitive, leaning on her parasol,
or appearing to lean on her parasol, but in truth a ghost without weight or weariness standing in perfect silence perfectly
still by the calm pool where the waterlilies are shutting their
blind bright eyes, Axel's mother being in blue, and blue leaves
falling, and the parasol a paler shade of blue, powder blue
perhaps, no, more transparent, watchet or skyblue or aqua-
marine, her parasol in its crochet shroud that paler beryl
colour, her parasol like a dream she has not yet quite succeeded
in dreaming, the whole scene her dream, a dream she has not

35

dreamt but will, all save the real silver buckles on her square-toed shoes, only the buckles on her shoes are real.

We are fortunate to be allowed within the garden . . . That is what Axel used to say to his mother. In one form or another he used always to deliver himself of this insincerity a little later, when they had left the garden, and the loud iron gates had clanged shut behind them. (He waited until later because, to be honest, the garden *bored* him while they were in it). They would usually be found sitting then in a poky restaurant where Axel was permitted, as a special dispensation, an ice of three different colours and tastes, in a tall green glass. Why he was granted the ice, then, he did not know. At no other time would his mother have dreamed of letting him eat an ice, because she said that they were bad for the teeth; but, after her cool blue trances in the garden, then, by some unspoken agreement between them, they went immediately to the dim restaurant— there was a cracked mirror on the wall behind the till, and the proprietress, a Madame Brangemore, said to be exiled royalty, did calculations on the mirror's surface with a lipstick—the restaurant where the waiter with the torn apron had prepared for Axel a fine religious ice of three flavours in a tall slim glass, and Axel would eat the ice with a long spoon and some wafer biscuit.

We are fortunate to be allowed within the garden . . . (A pompous, untruthful, flattering boy? A sycophant? A toad? Axel never supposed otherwise.)

His mother never agreed or disagreed. That was not her way. She would say: Eat your ice, don't you like it? Or: We shall be late if you do not hurry yourself just a little, my duck. Can't you take larger mouthfuls? Or: Honey, you really *must* learn how to sit properly on a chair in a restaurant.

Things of that sort, she would say. For some reason, she would never—Axel nearly said, answer his *question*, but then it was not a question, it was more a statement that wanted to call doubtful attention to itself. In any case, Axel's mother never would refer directly to what he said on that score,

36

making instead some trite critical reference to a this or a that or a shocking nothing, as he has tried to suggest.

Axel's mother, he hopes he has not given a contrary impression, was not indigenously, nor even eccentrically, American, in thought, or speech, or deed; except, perhaps, she had what Axel has noticed to be a habit amongst the better class of Americans, a habit of intelligent hopefulness of heart . . . It was not that she looked on the better side of things (though she did that too). It was that she expected well of a person because she trusted persons to answer at least the good in herself, answer it with the good in themselves, which she waited patiently to show itself to a shrewd gaze more than usually gifted with ability to detect the good, alert to its incidence, however strangely it might declare itself, however bizarre or reluctant its agents . . .

The oddest part of this is that Axel cannot recall his mother ever being wrong. She seems to have proved by her patience that one has only to wait long enough, and hope hard enough, rather wait and hope *openly* enough, for the good to work amongst us, to manifest itself in our doings with each other, and it will put in an appropriate appearance via even the most unlikely dramatis personae. Axel has learned this lesson, if he has learned it, by watching and knowing of his mother. He could not say that he has ever had the perseverance, or the inner calm, to see it shape forth out of his own experience. But then Axel has not his mother's American heart. Axel's heart is only half American. Axel's father was Welsh.

He was born in a valley in the north of Wales, Axel's father. Axel has never seen that valley, indeed he has never been to Wales in his life, it is not a place where there is much call for a man in his line, you might say. Yet Axel knows that valley as well as he knows the view there used to be from the window of the workroom in his Rome apartment (near the steps leading up to the house where Keats lay dying while Severn had troubles with the kettle boiling over), knows it better than that, maybe, certainly better than most of the dozens of windows he has lived by since, looking out or looking in. The reason Axel knows this valley so well is because his father used to play a game with him, oh it must have gone on until Axel was about nine or ten, a game that never, so far as Axel can remember, had a name, therefore he calls it simply The Game. This is how Axel and his father played The Game.

After tea, they always took tea quite Englishly, Axel would perch himself on the arm of his father's brown leather armchair and his father would say: Are you ready? Where's it to be today? And Axel would say, sometimes, Persia, or Cathay, or Thin, Sin, Sinae, or The Alleghenian Ridge. And to be sure he got fine stories if he said Persia or Cathay or Thin, Sin, Sinae, and a reasonable romance if he said The Alleghenian Ridge. But most often Axel would say: The Valley!

Then, supposing Axel had said the Valley, his father would take him on his lap and put his fingers over Axel's eyes, Axel remembers his father's fingers were sweaty and used to smell of tobacco from where he had been stuffing his pipe, and then his father would say, in a very quiet and gentle and precise voice, as if he was really a long way off and giving Axel directions over the telephone:

It is raining in the valley, the rain falls softly, on and on, it does not stop, it does not cease. Clouds, white clouds like smoke, are blown into the valley at its head, just by the black jaw of the mountain, and the wind holds the clouds in the valley so that it fills with mist and the mist rains, dusky rain, a snowing mist, rain all day, right from early this morning when you woke up and heard the rain on the roof, making the soft tattoo that was good to hear as you lay in bed, in the warm white bed under the humped coverlet of all patchwork colours, and you peeped out to watch the bright rain

38

running down the window, and the leaves all blurred beyond it, so that the window was one blur of green and silver, silver and green, the light travelling in the runningdown rain, and the brisk waking-up sound of raindrops splashing in the milk churn that serves the cottage as a waterbutt. When you got up you went to that blurred window and you opened it and what did you see? What! Have you forgotten already? Well there's memory for you! You saw a bird in the lilac. What sort of bird was he? A blackbird, that's what he was, boy, and he was preening his feathers a bit to get rid of the old rain, and the lilac was hanging all limp and damp and bedraggled, and you could smell it perfectly from the bedroom window, a death smell, perfect. The little brook in the valley, in the side of the valley, just by the house, was singing and making a chuckling noise in its stony throat, like a bee in a bottle, what with all the rain running out of the wood, drawn through the roots of the trees, and out of the steep fields, out of every particular brimming ditch and hole and sudden pool, and the brookwater flowing down fast, flowing fast down to the river that runs through the valley, in the floor of the valley. As you ate your breakfast, by the window above the waterbutt, the window that looks out into the blowing firs and the brown wood beyond, you could hear that little brook all the time, making a quick, fussy, sensitive sound, like a wristwatch, like a lady's wristwatch. And, after breakfast, you put on your coat and draped a good dry sack that smelt of meal round your shoulders, and you went out and enjoyed the tang of the sack as you walked proud and dry in the rain, and following the bulging brook down to the river, and when you were still a long way off, high on the perching ridges of the valley, you saw that the river itself was fat, swollen, full of muscle, running very fast, and that it was a new colour, a rackety deep-throated colour, almost yellow with the sand and silt and salt and earth and chalk it had tugged and ripped and bitten and sucked from the banks and would swirl down to sea with in its coursing. Yes, yes, a lion of a river, angry, iron and quick,

39

blood in its mane and round its mouth. Well, then, you got down to the river, down to the lion, down the slippery cage of the valley sides, and you saw that the bridge, the bridge made of old railway sleepers, blacktarred, wonky, that used to speak as you walked over it, and you sometimes to listen, and the tar sticking black to the soles of your sandals in summer, you saw that the bridge had been swept away in the night. And you saw tall logs reared up like stallions in the water, like fighting swans, and great tangled knots of logs, crested with filthy foam, smashed into the banks, wedged, jammed tight there, packed and quaking, and the ground shook all round where the river was running, the ground all around it shook with the shout of the river. Can you feel the ground shaking? Can you see the ruined river? That river is a wound that has opened in the world. Look in the river and you'll see all the pain you want to see, all the pain in the world, all the world's long wound, that was opened long ago but is new each time for you, your world, your wound, your river, your pain. Just look at it! You must be wicked to bleed like that.

Axel's father, you understand, had a sly Welsh accent, delicate and ceremonious, an accent apparent both in the rise and fall of his voice and the rise and fall of his thought. It lacked grammar, but not fire. When his imagination was kindled by an occasion like this he could be whimsical in a way Axel found, at the time, important and mysterious, warm and alert and fraught with the right mystery. That is to say, Axel did not understand all the lilt and rhetoric of his father's imagination, but he was in love with the colours of it, as much in love with that as he was in love with the vulcanite watch chain that made its loop across his father's belly.

And in the afternoon, Axel's father would go on, if they were playing this particular version of The Game, what did you do in the afternoon? You went into the brown wood, child, for it had stopped raining, and the sky was tall and blue, the sky was a going-on-for-ever blue, a kindly-meant lie, and you paused and you listened to the sound of raindrops dripping quicksilverly from leaf to leaf, and ferns bending straight again, and petals coming unstuck, and the suck of the earth, the good long suck of that drunkard earth. And you gathered bluebells, wet bluebells, pretty facts, which you carried home, you brought them home, an armful of wet blue flowers. You remember standing in the porch with them? looking at the clock? And then you took a chair from the kitchen, a plain, wooden, black upright-backed chair, and you set the chair comfortably in the porch and you sat there, for the mist was back at the valley's head, swirling, skirling, and it had begun to rain again, and your mother's hood was silvered with drizzle when she came back from market, and you sat on your dark wooden chair in the porch and listened to the rain, watching it fall across the valley, and you ate an orange and spat the pips, grasshoppers splashing in the grass that grew green to the very door. It began to get dusk, and a fog came up from the sea. The lights of the cars on the road to the mountains were blurred and furred and yellow in the far tilted bluegrey distance, like moths' wings curious against a pane. You watched them for a long time, until it was dark, then you went in and had your tea, a nice white egg in a scarlet eggcup, eaten with a silver apostle spoon, or perhaps it was a speckled egg in honour of the rain which had done you some honour, and certainly you had a crisp napkin that lay beside your plate and the napkin had a band round it and the band had a design of a snake on it, one snake swallowing its own tail, making a perfect circle of itself. When you had eaten your egg you folded the napkin and put it back in the snake, and then you sat by the logfire and read your book: THE MABINOGION.

That was your book, Axel's father would say, that was the book you read always. You read of Lludd and Llevelys, and of

Kilhwch and Olwen, and the dream of Rhonabwy, and of Peredur the son of Evrawc, and of the Lady of the Fountain, and of Rhiannon who rode on the pure white horse that never galloped, never went fast, always walked sleepily, like foam on a slow wave lolling to roll the long way home, yet outstripped the fleetest horses in the stables of Pwyll Prince of Dyved, until he called courteously, as a man should, for her to stay for him. And sometimes you watched the armies of sparks fighting in the chimneyback, at their sooty sparkling wars, and other times you heard the fire hiss as black spits of rain came gleaming down the long chimney open to the night. And you remember how once a thrush fell right down the chimney? yes, fell into the fire and then flew quickly out, round and about the room, its wings taut and alight, its feathers blazing, round and about, for its brief burning moment that seemed to you an illumination from another world, before it fell dead on the purple plush of the windowseat, a charred black little ball of feathers, which when you touched it fell apart to show clean neat white bone, tiny buds and knobs and hooks and bubbles of bone, bone that had been ready to show through the feathers of the burning bird before it was dead, which had ached to be free when it tumbled on the wind. You might remember that thrush again as you lie in bed, under the spangled coverlet, the rain stopped, the dark outstretched beyond the window like a hand saying no. Or you might think of owls that screech out in the night, those owls you are afraid of, winnowing down the moonbleached wheat, their feathers fringed with swarthy softness, cruel stares in love with the moon, and you a shrew or a vole among pineneedles on the dark floor of the wood. The prospect of your dreams might be amusing as you watch the candle, your nightlight, tower and fall on the bloodred curtain, and hear the hollow oak suffer the dissatisfied murmur of its few leaves, and its branches' archaic complaint, and also the sough of your parents' conversation downstairs, a long way away, your father and your mother, a long way away beyond any call

42

or hail that you might make, a long way away, too far away, as if on another shore, and you on the shore of sleep . . . But you know too that your dreams, when they come, as they will come, will not amuse you. Your dreams are never amusing.

You will dream, Axel's father would say, of the castle with the spiral stair, the starry stair that goes on and on, down and down, and you going down into deeper and deeper darkness, so that there's no end to darkness, only the infrequent respite of a tiny latticed window that gives onto a scene, beyond the moat of blood and the rainbow bridge, of startling star brilliancy, but which, if you should stay for comfort, soon is lost, changed, altered horribly, the big stars travelling mad across the sky to scribble words in a language you cannot read.

Or you will dream of the puppet theatre where you sit, and you are suddenly grown up, a man, with two, a dark fellow and a fair woman, and you are seized with cold fear pinching in the pit of your stomach, fear that you will fall from where you sit, topple over the slender golden rail of the balcony, falling down, down, down into the cavernous auditorium, so that you sweat and have to cling to the arms of your seat for very life, but the arms are wet, furry and slippery, the arms will not be held, they are snakes that whip you down, and the whole floor of the shelf of the theatre where you and the dark man and the fair woman sit now begins to tilt, to go forwards, to crack, to slide, so that you are slowly inching down tilting down towards the tiny bright stage far away below, though your companions seem not to notice, or not to care if they *do* notice, they remained engrossed in the puppet play, some kind of morality, or opera.

Or you will dream the dream in which you sit at a long low table in Haworth Parsonage, and Emily comes in from the moor with her dog, Keeper, and her merlin hawk, Hero, and Keeper is wounded and Emily cauterises his wound with the poker, and there is rain on her hair and on her hectic cheeks, and then she sits by the fire with you, shyly, on the horsehair sofa, and combs her hair with Maria's comb, but

43

the comb falls from her hand into the embers and burns, and then she drinks from a pint pot of your blood to strengthen her, but it is too late, and as she stands up to greet death eagerly as the only guest she was ever glad to see, the lines of her poem burn like the comb in your head :

> *There let thy bleeding branch atone*
> *   For every torturing tear:*
> *Shall my young sins, my sins alone,*
> *   Be everlasting here?*
>
> *Who bade thee keep that cursed name*
> *   A pledge for memory?*
> *As if Oblivion ever came*
> *   To breathe its bliss on me;*
>
> *As if, through all the 'wildering maze*
> *   Of mad hours left behind,*
> *I once forgot the early days*
> *   That thou wouldst call to mind.*

And at this point, or thereabouts, invariably, Axel would discover from the unpleasant pressure beneath his bottom, that his father had an erection.

Axel does not think his mother ever understood The Game; or, if she did, she did not approve of it, of the way Axel's father chose to play it, the actual content of the memory he would have imparted to his son. But Axel loved The Game, and he loved being in the Valley. Axel could never tire of it or forget a single detail of it. It was a great sorrow to him when his father stopped these performances, quite suddenly, at about the time Axel was ten. Axel remembers he had climbed onto the arm of the chair and was waiting expectantly for his father to put down his glass and begin. But his father only looked at him irritably and said, What do you want?

Axel was so startled that he fell off the arm of the chair. He would have gone away, as they say, with his tail between his legs, had The Game not meant so much to him, and had he not obscurely realised in that moment that his father's indifference threatened the whole fabric of his life as it then was.

Axel said: I thought we might play The Game tonight.

His father waved his hand. The white shirt at his wrist was like quick water cuffing a rock. You're too old for that now, he said.

That was all. A wave of the hand and it was gone, the Valley, Axel's childhood. It was over. His father's wrist dismissed it in its flowing collar of foam. Axel remembers it all perfectly and used to console himself with long thoughts of it.

But this was not the same.

Nothing was the same again.

From that time on, Axel's relations with his father worsened. He had little to say to Axel. Axel had nothing to say to him. Axel shut himself in his room when his father came into the apartment. At meal-times Axel looked elsewhere. He did not like the man he had to pass on the stairs.

Axel's father died when Axel was fourteen, and Axel could not weep.

He was shocked and angry at himself, bitterly, standing in front of the threefold mirror in his mother's bedroom and assuring himself that he would be damned for not being able to weep. His father was dead. The funeral was tomorrow. And he *should* weep. But it was no good. His eyes were perfectly dry and cold and clear, looking back at him from three faces. Then, after the funeral, Axel was proud; boasted of his tearlessness, of course.

Captain Rufus Coate

RUFUS COATE was the kind of explorer who only finds what he is looking for. Who can blame him if his Latin was not impeccable, the furrows he ploughed were not always straight, or the shoes he cobbled let in water? He was, in his shy way, a Catholic. We heard once, and from the right source too, that he had been excommunicated. Whether that particular pleasantry is true or not, he was at the time we knew him a sincerely if oddly *pious* man, rather more a missionary than a sea captain. He was, indeed, obsessed with what he called the dark places of the world. In his spartan cabin he had a great gaunt map, which was coloured part black, part white. The white parts were Christendom. The black places were heathendom. (We speak in his terms, you understand; it is not to be supposed that we share his opinions or beliefs; in any case, many places would have been surprised at their colour on Rufus Coate's map.)

This captain had made it his life's work to cancel out the black places *in imagination*. Nothing could please him more than when goodhumoured fancy permitted him to take a rubber to the shaded quarters of that critical map of the world's disposition. He did not do it often, he was not able to do it as frequently as he would have liked, but few things in life can have given anyone greater satisfaction than Rufus Coate got from this lucid duty, this definitive work, this illuminating mission. The habit dated from the day he had had the row with his mother. Rufus Coate called it *the* row because it was the only one he had ever had with his mother. He did not often speak of it, but when he did he said much, without

46

apparent pain or pleasure. From a hint here, a grimace there, it is possible for us to know precisely what happened, or at least to go over the scene as it continued to happen in his memory. The room had been filled with Captain Porteous's art treasures, there was a violin hanging from a nail in the wall, the eighteenth century wine-coolers contained flowering shrubs. His mother sat at her William and Mary writing table. Rufus sat on the floor in front of the fire. Captain Porteous was out riding Byron, cross as a snake. Poor Jennifer, we expect, was in Sussex. It had seemed a good moment to tell his mother that he was going to marry. In picturing the scene beforehand he had planned her delight. She would, as it were, welcome him into the ranks. She would be tender, reserved, a little sentimental. Their two prides would hold hands. But it was not like that. Mother, he said. His mother looked up abstractedly. She saw him, a mixture of boy and man, she saw him, she saw it all, the brilliant years at the Ecole Normale, the hard facts in his eyes, the penny on the shelf in her bedroom, the brutal libretto, the western windows crooked behind his head. She saw it all. The black poplars had grown. No detail eluded her. He had been her baby, a cripple, his women seven feet high, she had gone about closing cupboards for him, shutting all the doors, knocking on them, laughing. Now he paid her ten shillings a week for board and lodging. The room tilted slowly, his chair tilted, a shadow. Don't interrupt me now darling, she said, can't you see I'm busy? She went on with her sonnet. It seemed that there was not a single rhyme for 'scarce' in the English language. Rufus Coate, disconcerted, waited for her to finish. Then he told her that he was going to be married. His mother said, You must be mad. She started another sonnet, scrapping the one that had the word 'scarce' at the end of the second line. Ocean of Truth, she wrote, clasp me to your wide breast. But I'm going to be married, said Rufus, I've got to tell you, mother. His mother put down her pen. No, she said. What? said Rufus. You are

47

not going to be married, said his mother. She had risen, taking her pen with her. Now she fitted the cap on it. You are twentytwo, she said, she hasn't any money, your allowance will be stopped, and you needn't think you can go crawling to your grandmother; she won't give you a penny. Rufus Coate shut the mouth he had opened. He tried hard to understand. He felt vaguely that these words referred to him and that he ought to listen. But what did they mean? Who was this woman on whom his eyes rested without feeling yet who was capable of stirring some small recollection of gratitude in his kidneys? The light hurt his eyes. A little while ago the world had been clear enough. He felt his lips twitching. He smiled. He was now in a position to manipulate his life this way or that. He could bend it, like a playing card. His mother's gaze went from the flowering shrubs to the nailed violin, and back again. I have not loved flowers enough, she said. She went quickly from the room, her hand to her mouth, to shut out their perfume.

In his person, Rufus Coate was white with a waxen clearness. Beside ourself he looked like a sacramental taper next to a tallow candle. His character was companionably cold. He had never told a lie outside his business. He was so diffident that he appeared fragile, but in fact he was probably more enduring than granite, and his sense of humour was so strong that he once went into an undertaker's, lay down on the counter, clicked his heels together, and shouted, Shop! His smile was pink, his look was grey. There was a certain disproportion between the upper and lower parts of his face. His nose was less than Roman, more than Greek. His eyes were like blue milk, and small and mean and furtive. He was, we might suggest, an amateur of life. He kept his books on the shelves with their titles to the wall. He drank horse's blood for his anaemia. His diet consisted of brown bread husks specially baked in Warwickshire, boiled minced lean bullock's cheek, nightingales, brains, and Scone scones. His hair was red. His shoulders were broad, bowed. He smoked cigars as

48

though sucking food down a tube. He was of course celibate, but he had a woman-shaped bed.

We knew Rufus Coate, we may say well. We sailed with him on five voyages. The two of us burned words together. We talked long and late in those hours that are like no others, hours when the darkness around and above a ship is one with the darkness it moves through.

It was on one such night, a night off the Nore, a night of such stillness that in our memory of it we were like painted men on a painted boat idling on a sea of black paint, that he told us the story of his hero, Masterman Simple. He had asked us, over a jereboam of Rhenish and a piece of cheese that tasted like burnt milk, if we knew the story of the six roasted mice, the four cool keels, and the rhymes on the rock. We, wary of his distaste for rhyme, replied cautiously that no, we thought we had not heard that story. Nodding to himself with discriminating surprise, Rufus Coate told us as follows:

Jan Simple was a great man and a holy fool. I honour his memory. His lips were a wettened red, his cheeks white-golden like snow just stained by dogpiss. He wore a single earring and had a spade-shaped beard. His ears and nostrils were tufted with hair, his sidelocks were twisted into tight little curly horns. His eyes looked always as if they gazed at an old and sundrenched tenniscourt where the net sagged and the grass grew long and feathered; they filled easily with tears, not from emotion, rather as an overflow of the excess of lucidity within him. He spoke with a limp. His trousers were held up by a piece of string. He sported white ducks and a bow tie. He always ate fish on Fridays, not because he was a Catholic but so that there would be less for those who were.

One day this same Jan Simple conceived a plan to send out ships to Tierra del Fuego, to baptise the miserable aborigines. Sweet plan and plaintive . . . The year was 1839.

Simple sought for six months or more to find backers for

his watery crusade. To no avail. Then when all seemed lost, and particularly the aborigines, a midwife in Cheltenham gave him seven hundred pounds towards the endeavour. Her name was Mrs Tehuelche, and she wore a feather tippet. Simple had three hundred pounds of his own, which he had earned valiantly as a male prostitute in a village called Heap. (He was the *only* male prostitute in the Soke of Heap, hence the valour.) On this thousand smackers he set forth, game as a pebble, to wipe darkness from my map.

Now, obviously, Rufus Coate went on, Simple could not afford a schooner or a cutter or a clipper or a foist, but he had four cool-keeled boats built for him, at Candy Island, on the lines of those vessels in which Eirik the Red and his son, Leif the Lucky, discovered Greenland, and in which that little Welsh vagabond prince Madoc ap Owen Gwynedd[1] certainly did *not* discover America (though it is possible he reached Paradise) in the twelfth century. Two of these boats were powered by an apparatus which transmuted words into wind. This appliance was shaped somewhat like a tinfoil phonograph. Verbal items being fed into the huge funnel ear of it, its intricate guts—a thriving system of cogs and wheels, membranes and suspenders—divided each word into its component syllables, and each syllable into letters, and then extracted the *colour* of each letter and concentrated the colour values in what is sometimes called a verbomagnetic spectrum, releasing the thermonuclear content of the English language. It would

[1] For a cogent exposition of the anti-Madoc view, see Thomas Stephens' MADOC: AN ESSAY (London, 1893), so unfairly denied a prize at the Llangollen Eisteddfod held on September the twentyfirst, 1858. The subject for competition being announced, For the best essay upon the discovery of America in the twelfth century by Prince Madoc ap Owain Gwynedd, prize 20*l* and a silver star, and the judges being appointed, three wellknown Welsh *literati*—the Rev Thomas James (Llallawg), Myvyr Morganwg, and the Rev D. Silvan Evans, B.D., Mr Stephens sent in his essay under the *nom-de-guerre* of Gwrnerth Ergydlym. In this masterly piece of work he, in the words of his editor, Llywarch Reynolds, B.A. (Oxon.), presented an almost exhaustive summary of the literature of the subject, marshalling all the evidence usually cited for and against

50

only work on English words. And it was most effective with the words of English poets—particularly the Rowley forgeries of Thomas Chatterton. The following passage from that poet's BATTLE OF HASTINGS (ONE), for instance, was worth ten knots:

> *Howel ap Jevah came from Matraval,*
> *Where he by chaunce han slayne a noble's son,*
> *And now was come to fyghte at Harold's call,*
> *And in the battel he much goode han done;*
> *Unto Kyng Harold he foughte mickle near,*
> *For he was yeoman of the bodie guard;*
> *And with a targyt and a fyghtyng spear,*
> *He of his boddie han kepte watch and ward:*
> > *True as a shadow to a substant thynge,*
> > *So true he guarded Harold hys good kynge.*

These two boats were called the *Is* and the *Was*.

The other two boats were small bumboats. Not that Eirik the Red and Leif the Lucky had bumboats. But Simple had bumboats, two. For carrying vegetables and bibles.

Simple now set about assembling his crew. This consisted of six men chosen for their faith, their seamanship, and their skill in a particular line—one was a surgeon, one was a philosopher, the other four were Cornish.

In September 1840, in Swinburning weather, the seven went forth from Liverpool on the *Principia Mathematica*, out-

the Cambrian story, subjecting it to a rigid criticism, and finally adopting the negative view declared himself a disbeliever in the tale of

> *How Madoc from the shores of Britain spread*
> *The adventurous sail.*

What happened next has been described as rivalling in turpitude the disgraceful treatment accorded to Dewi Wyn o Eifion and his AWDL ELUSENGARWCH. Reynolds writes: Having become aware of the existence of the negative essay, the committee decided that the essay in question, being an essay not on the discovery but on the *non-discovery* of America by Madoc, was not upon the given subject, and must therefore be excluded from the competition. This unwarrantable interference with, and usurpation of the functions of, the judges, was warmly resented by those gentle-

51

ward bound for California. Their boats, loaded with six months' provisions and a petrary for shooting crucifixes, were stowed aboard. The gale aloft sung in the shrouds, the sparkling waters hissed before, and frothed, and whitened far behind. On the fifth of December they were landed on the dark improbable shore.

Now from the day when the *Principia Mathematica* sailed away to go round the Horn, no Christian eye saw Masterman Simple and his gallants again.

Imagine the situation, Rufus Coate invited. Seven venerable three-brained being-bodies, in four cool-keeled boats, gone out upon a weary waste of waters to convert a nomadic people whose numerals stopped at five, whose language they could not speak or read or understand, whose music made their hair stand on end, all in an archipelago singularly bare of food and spinsters. As if this was not bad enough, they discovered that the wind-word apparatus, essential to their progress, was too heavy for the boats, weighting them down and encumbering them in the water, so that they could go forward only slowly, and at a painful list, one mariner reading aloud from Chatterton's neglected masterpiece, AELLA, one thousand two hundred and fortyfive revolutionary lines that paved the garden path for Keats and Coleridge, while the others baled as studiously as they might. Also, the *Is* was illmade and soon sprung a galloping leak.

men, and Llallawg promptly resigned his office and declined to adjudicate. On the day before the Eisteddfod, the Rev D. Silvan Evans wrote to the secretaries in the following terms:

To the Secretaries of the Llangollen Eisteddfod

GENTLEMEN, I have read the essays on the discovery of America by Madoc ap Owain Gwynedd in the twelfth century with as much care and attention as the circumstances would permit, and the impression which the perusal of them has left on my mind is, that the existence of the socalled Welsh Indians has not yet been fully established, that Madoc's alleged discovery of the American continent rests upon bare conjecture, and that it is still an open question whether he ever left his native shores. If these essays may be con-

Nevertheless, the seven voyaged in grim and faithful pomp from island to island, from fog to snow, from mere absence to oblivion. They took light with them—that is the point of my story. That was Simple's point too. For, to be sure, he was a reader of Leibniz and Schleiermacher. I mean, the esoteric stuff in the letters to Arnauld[2] (which he had private copies of, rather before they were published), as well as the business of the windowless monads, the pre-established harmony, the identity of indiscernibles, and all that. Oh yes, he *knew*, did Simple. He knew what he was doing and what he was being, and what he was being doing and what he was doing being, and what was to be, and what was to be done. He was a metaphor, a type, a symbol, a flick of grace, a moral emblem in search of what it meant, an elucidator of obscurity. He was a crass disenchanted light moving into the darkness, going on and down through dirt and despair, down and on through despair and dirt, making black bright by his presence. The impervious nature of the language barrier, the scantness of the provisions, the ignorance of the women, the unsuitability of the boats, the (be it admitted) corrugated turgidity of some passages of AELLA—all this was as nothing to him. Suffering

sidered as exhausting the subject to which they refer, I can draw no other inference from their contents than that these points cannot, with our present stock of knowledge, be proved to the satisfaction of any unbiased mind. All the competitors, with one exception, adopt the affirmative side of the question, and defend it with greater or less ability, but Gwrnerth Ergydlym, *by far the ablest writer*, takes the opposite side. He examines the subject fully and candidly, and displays throughout a deep acquaintance with it, and no small amount of critical sagacity, and I cannot but regret that the promoters of the Eisteddfod should have deemed it their duty to exclude his masterly essay from competition simply because the author arrives at a

[2] e.g. In consulting the notion which I have of every true proposition, I find that every predicate, necessary or contingent, past, present, or future, is comprised in the notion of the subject, and I ask no more . . . The proposition in question is of great importance, and deserves to be well established, for it follows that every soul is as a world apart, independent of everything else except God, that it is not only immortal and so to speak impassible, but that it keeps in its substance traces of all that happens to it.

merely underlined the meaning. The more he suffered the more the meaning meant. That one man, one blunt man, one forked, fallible, tender man, that one Christian—or, rather, seven Christians, however tainted with Cornishness some of them were—by being in the dark places, by bearing their presence there among the heathen, which presence partook of Our Lord's absence, *made day where there was night before.* That was the meaning.

The natives, though cool, did not seem, at first, unfriendly. They had low brows, flat noses, loose skin, wide eyes, coarse hair, prominent zygomatic arches and tumid lips. Their heads and chests were disproportionately large, looking as though they belonged to another set. Sometimes they strolled down to the beaches on their slender outwardcurving legs and pelted the boats with precious stones before the seven could land, but more often they allowed them on their islands. However, not understanding the cross that was shown them, or the words that were spoken to them of that cross and in its name and sign and signature, they employed crucifixes for the humble office of toothpicks, and laughed at the Christians, and ignored them.

Then, during a thunderstorm when the sea began to squawk, both bumboats were lost, with the bibles and potatoes in them. During another storm, the anchors and the holy water went, also the tobacco. Next, they found that all their violins had

different conclusion from that of the others. As all the essays which assume the truth of Madoc's discovery, whether we take them singly or collectively, appear to me to fall far short of establishing the points which their respective writers have undertaken to prove, and as no other view of the subject is to be entertained, I hope I may be excused from pronouncing any opinion as to the comparative merits of these productions. I remain, Gentlemen, &c., &c.

This communication was suppressed by the secretaries, and no mention of it was made at the Eisteddfod itself. Reynolds observes that the Rev Silvan Evans was unable to be present at the Eisteddfod in consequence of severe domestic affliction, and that the other adjudicator, Myvyr Morganwg, who was present, and who had written an adjudication, was not allowed to read it. Instead, the Rev R. W. Morgan announced briefly

been left behind in the *Principia Mathematica*, and also Simple's prized viola de gamba, so they had no means of attracting penguins, bats, or sea-otters for food.

Thus wore away, bloodily, the harsh month of January, 1841. What marvel, if at length the mariners grew sick with long acceptance? They scarce could think of maintaining their quest, persevering in their duty, insisting on going forward with the light. It was enough, perhaps, to keep the light of themselves alive where they were. Simple beheld dark looks of growing restlessness. He heard distrust's low moan.

On the first day of February the *Is* was dashed on the rocks by a falling star, and proved unsalvable. Only the *Was* was left. Some of the crew fell ill of the scurvy. Some lived in a cave, that the boat could be used as a hospital for the others. A few fish and fowl were taken. A dead Yahgan baby was eaten surreptitiously. So March passed also. And then April, a cruellish month.

And so, said Rufus Coate, the Antarctic winter began, pitiless and giddy, with snow and ice to bless their veins and other troubles. From the middle of May they were all put on short rations, owing to the rapid whittling away of their six months' stores, depleted by the loss of what had been contained in the bumboats. At the end of June, one of the sadly confused Cornishmen, Brenzaida, died, worn out with Chatterton and scurvy. There is an entry in Simple's diary, dated about the end of June, enumerating the eatable items still left. Among them are the six mice. This is what he wrote about them:

that of the essays sent in, *one was not on the subject*; and of the others the judges could not decide which was the best, consequently, there would be no award. Let a contemporary newspaper report continue the tale:

Mr T. Stephens then stepped on the platform and claimed permission to say a few words in reference to the announcement made by Mr Morgan, but the chairman and Carn Ingli begged he would refrain from doing so, and Mr Morgan ordered the band to play up in order to drown the voice of the speaker. The audience, however, claimed a hearing for him, urged by Mr Francis of Manchester, who said it would be a burning shame to refuse a hearing to a man

The mention of this last item in our list of provisions may startle some of our friends, should it ever reach their ears, but circumstanced as we are, we partake of them with a relish, and have already eaten several. They are very tender, and taste like rabbit. Here is the recipe: Wash and trim your mouse, taking especial care to remove sinews from brains before blanching. Simmer till soft in salted water with butter and chopped seaweed. Drain and squeeze out excess liquids. Serve lukewarm and quickly.

In addition to the mice, a solitary king penguin, a dead fox, a half-devoured rainbow-fish flung up by the generous tide— all these pathetic fragments of life were seized on as rare treasure by the starving men.

When August arrived, with its heart like a parachute, the strength of all was nearly exhausted. One of the Cornishmen discovered a packet of garden seeds in the lining of his mackintosh and these were made into a kind of gruel. This, and mussel broth, was served to the invalids. Simple himself lived heroically by sucking mussels for a fortnight, until there was not even mussels left. He would have died then, and the others with him, had they not discovered a certain species of rockweed which proved edible and of some small value as sustenance. Unfortunately, this weed had the side effect of making

of Mr Stephens's literary reputation. The chairman yielded, and Mr Stephens then came forward. He had risen, he said, to protest against the terms of Mr Morgan's announcement. He had said that one essay was not on the subject. This was not correct. The essay was strictly to the point, and he would not hesitate to announce that the essay pointed at was that of Gwrnerth Ergydlym, of which he was the author. The real objection was that the conclusion arrived at was at variance with the preconceptions of the committee, and if they had manfully announced the fact, he would have made no remonstrance, but they had thrown dust in the eyes of the assembly, and committed an unfairness to him (hear, hear). He had, of course, seen that the committee held the affirmative view, but he had before denied, and continued to deny, that an Eisteddfod was to be an arena for special pleading, but rather for the promulgation of the truth, and he protested that no committee had any right to look upon their prizes as fees for the advocacy of onesided views of disputed

the genitals rot, but none of the mariners was willing to forego its consumption on that account (the philosopher, a Mr Bronstead, even swore that *he* felt better *without*).

On the twentythird, Mandel, the boatman, died, worn away with hunger and regret, and on the twentysixth another boatman, Heartpride, followed suit. Trollope, the remaining boatman, proceeded to go mad at the loss of his mates. Mr Bronstead, the philosopher, expounded to him the fundamentals of his idea—which he had been brooding over due to certain observations of the penguins—of a 'language game', a prefiguring, doubtless, of some sensible paragraphs in Wittgenstein's PHILOSOPHICAL INVESTIGATIONS. Mr Bronstead also found just sufficient strength to dig a grave for Mandel and Heartpride. Explaining to the interested Trollope that even such questions as *What is language?* and *What is the game?* cannot be finally answered, he took two sticks and made a pair of crutches, for Midshipman Simple was so weak he could hardly kneel to pray.

Simple and Trollope were soon the only two left in the cave, Trollope having murdered Mr Bronstead with certainties. Simple began to speak of dying in companionship—of getting back to the *Was*. He set forth with Trollope. But they were too weak and the winter too wild. They had to return to the cave.

Trollope, cherubic, unrepining, speaking volubly of love and the fine nappy ale of Kilmarnock, died on the second day

questions (hear, hear). The Madoc business had been under discussion for fifty years, and it was therefore not to be wondered at if the competitors took different sides. For his own part he treated it as an open question, and as the committee gave great prominence to the motto Y *gwir yn erbyn y byd* he was led to conclude that there was to be full liberty of discussion, and that their object was to arrive at the truth (hear, hear). In that spirit he had written. He said he was supported in his views by several of the ablest historical critics in Wales, by the late Mr Humffreys Parry, the Rev Thomas Price (Carnhaunawc) and the Rev Walter Davies (Gwallter Mechain). His ambition, he said, was to be the interpreter of the claims of the language and literature of the Principality to neighbour-

of September. His last words were, The polar bear and the tiger cannot fight. (A truth later plagiarised by Freud, if truth is capable of plagiarism.)

Jan Simple was now helpless. There was no Trollope left to shut his wild wild eyes with kisses four. Besides, the remains of his genitals were in a sorry state. Passion on the third and the fourth, passion on the fifth and the sixth. No food. No hymns. Nothing. Just enough vitality to write a few lines on a paper which he hoped might one day reach Mrs Tehuelche in Cheltenham. And all the time, the one long grind to stay alive, not—I am sure of it—from any craven or even reasonable fear of death, but to keep the light there just a little longer in the cave, just another day, just another hour, just another minute, for when he died it would go out and the place would be black again, and he knew it.

It is to be supposed, Rufus Coate went on, that Masterman Simple died on the evening of the sixth of September, St Bega's Eve.[1] But no one can be sure, for there was none to make record of his passing. Nor can we know if the only other member of the unlucky crew, Mr Handyside, the surgeon, died before or after his captain. He had remained in the *Was*. It is probable that the difference of date could not amount to much. The transitive adventure was over.

ing and continental nations, he had hitherto done so to the best of his ability, and had the satisfaction to find that he was considered to be an honest exponent of wellfounded claims, and he would still continue to urge strongly and persistently every merit honestly pertaining to the history and national character of the Kymry (hear, hear). But he thought it lowered them as a people to be arguing claims which they could not prove, and that they were only clouding their own reputation in attempting to deprive Christopher Columbus of the fame to which he was justly entitled (hear, hear). He, for one, would be content with simple truthfulness, he would never be a jackdaw decked out with borrowed feathers, but would be content with his own plumage, brilliant or plain as that might be (hear, hear). He then concluded by entering his protest against the announcement made by Mr Morgan as being that of the committee and not of the judges, as being in itself untrue, and as being at variance with what

[1] Virgin, seventh century. Alias St Bees.

When Captain Mott, in Her Majesty's ship *Logick*, touched at last at that spot—as he had been given permission by the Government to do, at the solicitation of Simple's creditors— various writings in verse, limericks inscribed on the rock, guided him from place to place, until on the twentyfirst of January, 1842, he came upon the wreck of the *Is*. Then he found the unburied bodies of Simple and Trollope in the cave. Then a packet of papers and books, testimony to the light that had failed. Then the *Was*, with the windword machine, and the seastained copy of THE COMPLETE POETICAL WORKS OF THOMAS CHATTERTON.

Only one of the limericks is worth quoting :

> *There was a young student at John's*
> *Who wanted to bugger the swans,*
>   *Whereupon said the porter:*
>   *Sir, pray take my daughter—*
> *The birds are reserved for the dons.*

Captain Mott wrote : Their remains were glued together and planted close to the spot, and the funeral service read by Lieutenant Dodwell. A lewd inscription was placed on the rock, the colours of the boats and ships were struck half mast, and three volleys of musketry were the only tribute I

he knew from private information to be the opinion of the adjudicators (applause). Carn Ingli (the Rev J. Hughes, one of the secretaries of the Eisteddfod—the other being the Rev John Williams, Ab Ithel) then replied that Mr Stephens was under a misapprehension. The announcement was not intended to be final, and he gave a pledge to have the decision reconsidered. Mr Stephens said there was no reservation in the first announcement, but since they had promised to reconsider the subject, he would, pending that decision, withdraw his protest.

Reynolds observes, however, that the Llangollen committee could not be induced to do what was right in the matter of this competition, and the prize was never awarded.

In partial support of the opposing view—that Madoc may have found his way to America—this item from the *South Wales Daily Post* for January the fifteenth, 1914, may be of interest :

could pay to this loftyminded Englishman and his saltfaced companions.

When Rufus Coate had finished telling us Simple's story he was so desperately shaken it was as if he had prepared his soul before us for our banqueting. Indeed, we were ourselves stirred up to such a degree that you might have been forgiven for supposing that the terrible tale had touched somewhere on the innermost secrets of our own biography. We sat in silence a long while, listening to the ship creak where she rode on a lank anchor, waiting for the tide which would bear us up the Thames to the Pool.

At last, the captain turned to us, his eyes refreshed with pity, and offered, when we were dead, for our patience in hearing him out, to pour a bottle of whisky on our grave each year on the occasion of our birthday.

We thought this uncommonly decent, and said so.

Best Talisker highland malt, he said.

Thanks, we said.

Rufus Coate hesitated as a thought came. Then he said : Of course it will be passing through my kidneys first.

A word or two more about Captain Rufus Coate. He was of a thoroughly musical disposition. When he was six his hands hung long as Lincoln's from his cuffs, and he could already

WELSH INDIANS

Circumstantial Story

MEDICINE MAN'S QUIET SPOOF

Preferred a Wigwam to Palace

Mr Joshua Hughes, Rhosygadair, Cardigan, who takes a keen interest in the question of the Welsh Indians, writes to say that some time ago he wrote to the editor of *Y Drych* enclosing a copy of an article which originally appeared in the *Greal* in 1805, and asked his views on it.

play the glass harmonica. His early experiences included a vision of Our Lady, who performed a striptease of flesh before his innocent startled eyes—peeling off bits of herself here and there until she was all skeleton, the cultivation of a new flower (of the insectivorous variety) called a whimsy, a walking-on role in a pantomime in which the Principal Boy developed Lesbian opportunities during an arbour scene, to the delight of the Principal Girl but scandalising three burghers filling the difficult parts of oaktrees and causing an elderly nymph to perish of heartfailure after whirling about the stage like a dervish for three minutes twentyeight seconds, shrieking Horrors of Nature, Hell, and Death! and an experience he never gave us details of, in Kew Gardens, with a Welsh Indian called Keenstroke.

At the age of twelve he was master of the bugle, the archlute, the psaltery, the rebeck, the dulcimer, the seraphina, the shawm, the flageolet, and a special humming top in C which he had patented himself and which sounded a tune somewhere near Einna's LOVE IS LIKE THE WILD ROSEBRIAR[3] when set to work on the flat end of an empty Bulmer's ciderbarrel in E. He played with Dame Nellie Melba at the age of sixteen. He was then of the opinion that the great American firefly should be imported into Spain to catch mosquitoes. By the time he

The Article

The article was as follows:

Lieutenant Roberts' account of his interview with a chief of Welsh Indians, translated by Mr T. Roberts from the *Greal*, printed in 1805:

In the year 1801, being at the City of Washington, in America, I happened to be at an hotel smoking my cigar, according to the custom of the country, and there was a young lad, a native of Wales, a waiter in the house, and because he displeased me by bringing a glass of brandy warm instead of cold I said to him jocosely in Welsh, I will give you a good beating. There happened to be at the time in the same room one of the secondary Indian Chiefs, who on my pronouncing those words rose up in a great hurry, stretching forth his hand, asking me at the same time in the ancient British tongue,

[3] W. Marriott and Sons, 1879.

reached his majority, it would have seemed that his career was steady before him for the rest of his life—composing, translating Wagner, eating, perhaps (as he said jovially) cribbing bits of Schoenberg's PIERROT LUNAIRE for grisly exploitation in the hit parade. But then, all at once, on the eve of his twentyfirst birthday, he was suddenly 'smitten' with a desire to transform the playing of theatre-organs into an art.

It was while playing, to the accompaniment of a shifting diaphan of lights and the burbling of two silver fountains, J. S. Bach's CHROMATIC FANTASIA AND FUGUE IN D MINOR on the organ at the Odeon, Southend, that he began the unfinishable smile over the shoulder which led to his nervous breakdown and made it necessary for him to wash his mind and heart clean of musics, and go to sea.

About the same time he first read of Masterman Simple. Practical experience now led him always to go out with bowler and umbrella during the rioting season. These emblems were recognised by the police. A colleague, as he pointed out, who sallied forth hatless and wearing a tweed jacket, was promptly arrested and put in a Black Maria. A seamless idealist, Rufus Coate was never arrested. Indeed, he was so lucky that, as someone once said, if he had been dropped in the Irish sea he would probably have popped up with a U-boat under each arm. After keeping a brothel in Orleans, he served for a while

Is that their language? I answered in the affirmative, shaking hands at the same time, and the chief said that it was also his language and the language of his father and mother and his nation. I said to him, So it is the language of my father and mother and also of my country. Upon this the Indian began to inquire whence I came. I replied I came from Wales, but he had never heard a word about such a place. I explained to him that Wales was a principality in a kingdom called England. He had heard of England and of the English, but never of such a place as Wales. I asked him if there were any traditions amongst them whence their ancestors had come from. He said there was, and that they came from a far distant country, very far in the East, and from over great waters. I conversed with him in English and Welsh. He knew better Welsh than I did, and I asked him to count in Welsh. He immediately counted to a hundred and more. He knew English very well, as he was trading with the

in Algeria. It happened that the two regular conductors of the Radio France Symphony Orchestra, living there in exile for the duration, supported opposing political factions; at each rehearsal, therefore, one half of the orchestra walked out chanting slogans. For Coate this was the last straw. At the time when we knew him he was finished with music. The only occasion on which we ever saw him truly angry was when he reprimanded a cabinboy for whistling Monteverdi's ZEFIRO TORNA.

As to the circumstances of his excommunication—if he *had* been excommunicated—these were said to involve his carrying pistols into Notre Dame, on purpose to shoot the choir. So far as he was concerned, any sort of song made a dark place, and had to be cancelled out.

Even birdsong was abhorrent to him—which was one of the reasons why he went to sea, the mewing of seagulls being perhaps the least 'musical' of all birdcalls known to us.

This hatred he rationalised thus : music, being a complete and selfconsistent language of feeling, is necessarily meaningless; indeed, strictly speaking, there is no music outside us, *music when it is played plays us*; Bach and Beethoven and Bartók were therefore hungry men, and they still feed on the human spirit . . . Music, in his estimate, gnawed at the vital parts of us, bled us of our substance in tempting us to finish its cadences with words of our own, was always motherly,

English Americans. Amongst several things I asked him how was it they retained their language so well from mixing with the language of other Indians. He answered that they had a law, or an established custom, forbidding any to teach their children any other language until they were twelve years of age. After that they were at liberty to teach any language they liked. I asked him if he would like to go to England and Wales. He said he had not the least inclination to leave his native country, that he would rather live in a wigwam than in a palace. I was astonished and greatly annoyed when I saw and heard such a man, who had his face painted with yellowish red and of such appearance, speaking the ancient British language as if he had been brought up at the foot of Snowdon. His hair was shaved excepting round the crown of his head and there it was very long and neatly platted, and on the crown he had placed ostrich

63

demanding, destroying or disturbing of our wholeness. Nor was this a criticism that could be answered by recourse to simplicity. The simplest melodies, he used to point out, were the biggest monsters, for didn't they demand to be interpreted in the light of all their probable harmonies? Music was a malignant multiplication of the cells of sound. Music was cancer of the memory. We think he saw composers as witches who had stuck pins in images of the human heart and voice. Certainly, one or two notes struck formally on a pianoforte affected him like blows in the brain. A performance of Schubert's DEATH AND THE MAIDEN, played for him after dinner once by a schoolmistress in Millom and her friends, and which he had perforce to sit out for courtesy and honour's sake, left his trunk and legs mottled with thundercoloured bruises and his urine smelling of violets.

That is enough for now about Rufus Coate.

feathers. These Indians are about 800 miles southwest of Philadelphia according to his statement, and they are called in general Asgnaws or Asgnaw nation. The chief courted my society astonishingly seeing we were descended from the same people. He used to call upon me almost every day and take me to the woods to show me the virtues of various herbs which grew there, and which were best for all sorts of fevers, for he and his kindred were acquainted with compound medicine.

JOSEPH ROBERTS
Formerly of Hawarden, Flintshire.

Supporters of Stephens

The editor *of Y Drych* wrote to say it was out of the question to secure any further information relative to the Welsh Indians, and that the story about the Welsh Indian at Washington was unreasonable on the face of it, as well as the stories in *Drych y Prif Oesoedd,* etc. He added that in his opinion the views of Mr Thos. Stephens, of Merthyr, were pretty near the truth.

Howell

SAPPHO'S STEPFATHER, the Count C, was a little man, meagre, milkfaced, bat-eared, bony, somewhat bandy legged but in no sense muscular or given to physical exercises. He invariably looked as if he would die if he had to utter another three words. In fact, his health was perfect; he was strong as a ferryman. He certainly never caught one of the debilitating and feverish colds which have afflicted poor Sappho all her life and which were an especial curse during her adolescence. He had a face like a wet puddingbag, and smiled habitually: prim, bloodless, disapproving lips. His face as a matter of fact was slightly too loose for his smile, rather more than was adequate to contain it, that is, like the skin of a tangerine. He was an extremely sensual person: nuns, Welch fusiliers, orchids, it was all one to him. He had the squint of a weasel and the stoop of a clerk. A student of those who have extended or diverted theological tradition by their heresies, he was himself the kind of saint who blesses the beggar he refuses a penny to. He did not believe or disbelieve in one God.

Sappho, whose breasts are like boiled eggs with the shells just off, remembers that her stepfather had a peculiar interest in, and affection for, the Victorian 'card', friend of Rossetti, purveyor of smut to Swinburne: Charles Augustus Howell. The Count knew more about this 'somewhat mysterious personage' than anyone Sappho has ever met. He also knew much more than he would tell, and much more than Sappho has ever been able to discover about Howell from any memoirs of his period, or dictionaries of biography, or the innumerable and equally tedious lives of Rossetti.

Howell was in some respects the only *relevant* character of his time—though, in looking long at Rossetti's sketch of her asleep over a copy of THE DEFENCE OF GUINEVERE, Sappho confesses she has sometimes been tapped on the shoulder by half a hope that there was a spark of something or other in Jane Morris.

Howell claimed to be a Portuguese, descended from the Marquis de Pombal. His father is said to have been a drawing master in Lisbon. Sappho discounts the opinion that he was any descendant of James Howell, that priggish little clerk of King Charles's council, whose EPISTOLAE HO-ELIANAE was always on the table beside Thackeray's bed.[1] Rossetti wrote:

> *There's a Portuguese person named Howell*
> *Who lays on his lies with a trowel;*
> *Should he give over lying*
> *'Twill be when he's dying*
> *For living is lying with Howell.*

One of his better poems.

However, not all Howell's life was a lie; some of his activities were in the faded service of truth, though at this distance, and given the lack of sympathy and understanding he met from his circle, it is hard to sift and assess this.

In his youth he had been mixed up in a plan to assassinate Napoleon the Third. This was in collaboration with Felice Orsini. They threw three bombs at the emperor's carriage as he was on his way to the opera. The bombs missed. Napoleon was unhurt. Several other people were killed or wounded, amongst them Orsini. Howell escaped to graduate as a brigand in the fortress of the Serras da Estrella.

---

[1] Presumably because it contains (vol. ii, Letter 56, p. 354; 4th edition, 1673) the following: But, my Lord, you would think it strange, that divers pure *Welsh* words should be found in the newfound World in the *West Indies*. Yet it is verified by some Navigators; as *grando* (hark), *nef* (heaven), *lluynog* (a fox), *pengwyn* (a bird with a white head), with sundry others which are pure British.

He had dived for gold to Spanish galleons.

He had written a monograph on the case of Lieuben, the German gambler, who wagered that he would succeed in turning up by chance a pack of cards in a certain order stated in written agreement, and who turned the cards and turned the cards ten hours a day for twenty years until after 4,246,028 complete operations he succeeded.

He had been chief engineer of the Badajos Railway.

He had belonged to the Order of the White Rose and was a Knight Commander of the Portuguese Order of Christ.

He had served a sentence for a joy he did not commit.

He had dealt in holy water.

He had been sheik of a tribe of outlaws in Morocco.

He had been a listener to Beethoven's STRING QUARTET NUMBER FOURTEEN IN C SHARP MINOR, OPUS 131.[1]

He had been a page to the Pope.

He had sold silver for the real Roger Tichborne.

He had married his cousin Kate.

He had been convicted of cardsharping in Portugal before he came to Darlington at the age of seventeen, to be apprenticed to Stephenson, the great engineer.

He had worked as Rossetti's agent, selling paintings and making him a packet. He had also dealt with the draughts at Kelmscott.

He had bought the body of a tramp named Howell Murray who died in Paddington Hospital in 1878, and had him buried in a brand-new family vault as Sir Murray Howell Murray, Bart, my wife's father.

Now, Sappho, whose mouth is redder than the pimpernel, doesn't think Rossetti's friends ever understood his love for Howell. In her DANTE GABRIEL ROSSETTI: HIS FRIENDS AND ENEMIES, Helen Rossetti Angeli quotes from an unpublished letter to her uncle in which Burne-Jones calls Howell a base, treacherous, unscrupulous and malignant fellow. (He must be

[1] Zusammengestohlen aus Verschiedenem Diesem und Jenem—Beethoven to Schott, his publisher.

wicked to deserve such praise!—as Browning *almost* said on
another occasion which maybe involved him.)

Swinburne's epitaph described him choicely : That polecat
Howell . . . the vilest wretch that I, at all events, ever came
across. Watts said to me once—Howell ought to be flayed
alive (not with reference to any matter concerning Gabriel).
And, by God, if I could have sentenced him to be whipped to
death I would have done so. I am not sure that I would not
now, if he were not (happily) in that particular circle of
Malebolge where the coating of eternal excrement makes it
impossible to see whether the damned dog's head is or is not
tonsured.

Mr Swinburne also delighted in the pornographic books and
drawings Howell had provided him with, and quite possibly
at one time employed him to fill the Muse's rôle of flagellant
schoolmaster. After his old friend was dead he wrote a couplet
in memoriam :

> *The foulest soul that lived stinks here no more.*
> *The stench of Hell is fouler than before.*

Madox Brown referred to Howell as one of the biggest liars
in existence, the Munchausen of the Pre-Raphaelite circle.
He said the man was halfmad.

Georgie Burne-Jones contented himself with the acid brush-
off : He was a stranger to all our life meant. Ergo, says Sappho,
their life had little meaning. In any case, the Burne-Joneses
could not have been expected to keep up with Howell. On
the occasion of his first visit to their house he arrived late and
dishevelled, explaining that his hansom cab had collided with
another, that the cabbies had fought and he had thought it
proper to exchange cards and apologies with the person in
the other hansom. I handed him my card, said Howell, and
he gave me his. And just imagine my astonishment—I have not
yet recovered from it—here is the card he handed me. He
showed them the card. On it was written : Charles Augustus
Howell.

Theodore Watts-Dunton wrote : If he had possessed a private income, and if that income had been carefully settled upon him, I believe he would have been one of the most honest of men; I know he would have been one of the most generous. This, in Sappho's opinion, is Pines talk, for it implies that Howell was neither honest nor truly generous and that he was out for what he could get. No less an authority than T. J. Wise, in any case, said Howell earned his living by selling forged Old Masters.

Howell's classicism is perhaps most evident in the fact that he once put fifteen initials after his name on a School Board circular, making Rossetti write to him : I assure you they are likely to produce an injurious impression.[1]

The source of much hatred of Howell is his part in the recovery of poems from Mrs Rossetti's coffin. That disinterment, unique in the history of English poetry, took place at Highgate Cemetery on the night of the 10th of October, 1869. Howell was there to oversee, wearing a squeaky pair of shoes. The others present were Henry Virtue Tebbs, a solicitor; and a Dr Williams, of Camberwell. A party of workmen did the digging by the light of torches and a bonfire made at the graveside. When the coffin had been opened, Howell took out the book of poems and gave it to Dr Williams to disinfect. It was Howell who reported that Lizzie's (Elizabeth Sidal's) hair was still miraculously golden, encouraging Rossetti to write :

> *Even so much life hath the poor tress of hair*
> *Which, stored apart, is all love hath to show*
> *For heartbeats and for fireheats long ago:*
> *Even so much life endures unknown, even where*
> *'Mid change the changeless night environeth*
> *Lies all that golden hair undimmed in death.*

It is possible that Howell told the truth on this occasion.

Howell visited Rossetti on his deathbed and made him

---

[1] The old Cockney wop !—Sappho.

laugh. He was the last person to do so, which is some merit. Mrs Angeli reports that their conversation went as follows:

Rossetti: What are you doing now?

Howell: Buying horses for the King of Spain.

Rossetti's secretary, Henry Treffry Dunn (pronounced Cornishly thus, Tre*ff*ry, with the stress on the second syllable, as he was at some pains to point out to Howell on the occasion of their first meeting at Howell's house in Brixton) wrote once:

When Howell joined us unexpectedly in the studio, the flow of talk became lively. Howell had a lot to say, and it consisted of the most astounding experiences and adventures he had gone through. He had just left Whistler, and was full of a Long Eliza he had picked up somewhere, of his etching of old Battersea Bridge, of which he had been shown a proof, and of his latest witticism. The main object, however, of Howell's visit was to get from Rossetti a drawing he had made of a lady. I infer some bargaining had been going on between them, and that the drawing formed part of the bargain, but as Rossetti prized it highly, to gain possession of it was not a very easy matter and required much diplomacy. I now had an opportunity of looking over and admiring a series of Rossetti's first ideas and sketches for many of his pictures, and studies of heads, which were contained in a large, thick book, lying on a little cabinet in a distant corner. It was a great and unexpected treat to see this collection, a most varied one, amongst which were many carefully finished likenesses, some in red chalk, and others in pencil and in pen and ink, including pencil sketches of John Ruskin (not bearded then), Robert Browning, Algernon Charles Swinburne, William Morris, and other wellknown men. At last we came to the page at which the drawing Howell had come to secure was affixed. It was a beautiful face, delicately drawn, and shaded in pencil, with a background of pale gold. Howell, with an adroitness which

70

was remarkable, shifted it from the book into his own pocket, and neither I nor Rossetti ever saw it again.

Now this story has been overlooked by Rossetti's biographers. That is, according to Sappho its significance has been overlooked. What does it mean? It means that Rossetti and Howell had been in dispute over a drawing by Rossetti of an unknown lady of great beauty, that Howell had demanded the portrait as part payment of a debt, or in fulfilment perhaps of some other more complicated sort of bargain, that Rossetti had proved difficult, and that Howell had consequently chosen to take the picture from him in public *so that Rossetti had no chance of stating his real reasons for not wanting to part with it.*

Sappho, whose eyelids are like little boxes of mother-of-pearl, is going to return to this incident later. Here let it suffice to say that the Count C's interest in that drawing was obsessive. He would spend hours brooding over the story, tapping his fingers on the table, other hours flicking through all the available portfolios of Rossetti's work, in search of some hint of the beautiful girl, delicately drawn, and shaded in pencil, with a background of pale gold, which he knew he would never find there.

Now here is another relevant passage from Dunn, which Sappho has by heart. You must pardon her for quoting such barber's assistant's prose, but we are none of us concerned with 'style', she hopes.

Howell, he writes, wanted to show me a bit of old oak carving in Rossetti's bedroom, which I thought a most unhealthy place to sleep in. Thick curtains, heavy with crewel work in seventeenth century designs of fruit and flowers (which he had bought out of an old furnishing shop somewhere in the slums of Lambeth), hung closely drawn round an antiquated fourpost bedstead. It had belonged to his father and mother, and he had been born in it. A massive panelled oak mantelpiece reached from the floor to the ceiling, fitted up with numerous shelves and cupboardlike recesses, all filled with a medley of brass repoussé dishes, blue china vases filled with peacock feathers, oddly-fashioned early English and foreign candlesticks, Chinese monstrosities in bronze, and various other curiosities, the whole surmounted by an ebony and ivory crucifix. The only modern thing I could see anywhere in the room was a Bryant and May's match box! On the other side of the bed was an old Italian inlaid chest of drawers, which supported a large Venetian mirror in a deeply-carved oak frame. Two or three very uninviting chairs, that were said to have belonged to Chang the Giant—and their dimensions seemed to warrant that statement, as they took up a considerable amount of space —and an oldfashioned sofa, with three little panels let into the back, whereon Rossetti had painted the figures of Amor, Amans, and Amata, completed the furniture of the room. With its rich, dark green velvet seats and luxurious pillows, this sofa looked very pretty and formed the only comfortable piece of furniture visible. The deeply-recessed windows, that ought to have been open as much as possible to the fresh air and cheerful garden outlook, were shrouded with curtains of heavy and sumptuously-patterned Genoese velvet. On this fine summer's day, light was almost excluded from the room. The gloom of the place made one feel quite depressed and sad. Even the little avenue of limetrees outside the windows helped to reduce the light, and threw a sickly green over everything in the apartment. It was no wonder poor Rossetti suffered so much from insomnia!

O galloping dreary Dunn. Worried about the comfort of the sofa, the chairs, bullying and blustering away within himself like a charlady that the windows should be opened, the lime trees cut down. What an idiot! Depressed and sad indeed! Did he not turn round from his selfpreoccupied trivia-seeking misery at any time to observe *what Howell was doing behind him with the Chinese monstrosities in bronze*? And did he have no inkling of the significance of the figures Howell had told him represented Amor, Amans, and Amata?

No, depressed and sad, he saw nothing. Sappho thinks that

this is true, although she cannot quote Dunn without reserve—
i.e. without care—lest she should drop into what she desires
to avoid; and that is fiction. Certainly Dunn did not for
a moment suspect Howell's purpose in bringing him into
the green room. He treated the Bryant and May's matchbox
to an exclamation mark, but not to the examination it would
have repaid.

He goes on, and this is the point of Sappho's quoting such
a ninny : A few pictures, not of a very cheerful description,
hung on the walls where there was space. One, I remember,
was particularly gruesome. It represented a woman all forlorn
in an oar-and-rudderless boat, with its sail flapping in the wind
about her, alone on a wide expanse of water. In the distance
was a city in flames over which the artist had inscribed *The
City of Destruction*. In the sky were numerous winged dragons
and demons, whilst swarming around were horrible sea-monsters, all intent upon upsetting the boat. It was not a bad
picture as far as finish and colour went, but the subject was
too dreadful.

Perhaps Sappho should take this as epigraph to her story?
The subject was too dreadful. The verdict of a Dunn upon
us all.

Howell was murdered in 1890.

His body was found in a Chelsea gutter.

His throat had been cut.

Between his teeth a half-sovereign was clenched.

His murderer has never been discovered.

After his death there was a three days' sale of his effects at
Christie's. According to one account he came from his grave in
Brompton Cemetery and attended it. Mr L. H. Myers had
challenged the accuracy of the description of one lot, pointing
out that the hair in a locket which purported to be that of
Mary Queen of Scots could not be hers as it was the wrong
colour. Howell led Myers aside after the lot had been sold and
taken away from the saleroom, and explained with many a
digression that he was quite right, the relic had been dropped,

c*

the hair lost, and he had put into it some of Rosa Corder's hair instead, and that nobody, he was quite sure, possessed sufficient historical acumen to detect the fraud.

Now the Count C, Sappho need hardly say, also knew these passages of Dunn's book by heart. Sappho must have heard them recited on at least three occasions, in his puritanical falsetto. Yet it is only lately that she began to understand them. As for the Count, he *never* understood them, that Sappho is sure of. Sappho remembers how she tried once to commit suicide. When the Count caught her he said, What would your precious God think if He met you that way, eh? Answer me that! Sappho thought it no time for conundrums and found it difficult to comply; but she did, eventually. She was struck by the Count's looming appearance in the silver side of the little spirit lamp she used at table. One of her ancestors fought as two persons in the English Civil War, by day a gay Roundhead, by night a Cavalier.

Before Sappho talks of the not-bad-picture-whose-subject-was-too-dreadful, it occurs to her that you may not fully have comprehended Dunn's reference to the uninviting chairs that were said to have belonged to Chang the Giant. Sappho perceives that you are in some small difficulty over the matter: *Who is Chang the Giant?* She must not let such a question loom unanswered in your mind or you will be in no fit state for hearing out the rest of her story. Sappho wants you to listen to the storying, not the story, as she has told you, and if she does not here append some words to clarify Dunn's reference to Chang you may lose that which is essential to all of us—your politeness, the ease of your disposition towards her.

Of Chang, therefore. Chang was known also as the tall man of Fychow. He made his first appearance in London in the autumn of 1865, borne in a silver rickshaw pulled by fifteen negresses to the Egyptian Hall, in Piccadilly. Dressed

74

in white satin trousers and a zephyr, sitting like a stone joss upon a throne, accompanied by his wife and his dwarf, he made the following speech:

Fellow haemophiliacs, name of Chang. I am by birth a householder of Fychow, in the Auhwy quarter of the earthly lodgment of the Chinese empire. I am by profession a barber of nature. The Changs have all been great (tall) men. My father, Chang Tzing; my grandfather, Chang Chow, master of significant images, composer of illtempered scherzos for the hammerclavier; my greatgrandfather, Chang Chun, the man of war, the cause of resurrection in others, of whose great deeds our poets love to sing: all were great (tall) men, of whom I am the last and least, the poor and humble, the stunted and crouched and superficial representative. My elder brother, Chang Sou Gow, is a firstclass private in the Imperial Army, at Foo-Chow-Foo. He is in height six inches under me, but in massiness I cannot compare with him. He weighs thirtythree stones. He is known as the Public Diamond, the terror of the Tartar, before the singlehanded clap of whose hand the rebel flies. Already the Footow of Foo-Chow-Foo has conferred upon him the honorary title of Cheen Chung, leader in battle of a thousand men, and wearer of the mandarin's blue button.

I have one sister living, Chen Yow Izn. She is wed and well, gives her leisure to the poor, knits and hunts, yet is only seven feet tall.

My derelict mother lives (derelict only in the extravagance of her modesty, for I hasten to add that she claims my first duties, with my mistresses—for who can serve his rulers who has been negligent in his duty to his parents?). She is of ordinary household size. And thus her family stands: Chang Sou Gow the Brave, myself the Tall, and Metzoo my sister, the Domestic Jewel.

75

As a boy, I resembled the pyramids. My games were as follows: Civilisation, Semi-Pelagian Heresies, As You Like It, Simplicity, Urge, Similar Feasts, and I Dare Say. When I was old enough I went to school, and was educated in agony, logomachy, obstinacy, and the metaphysics of Sham, studying with especial care the example of Occam, Napoleon, and Richard Cromwell, and specialising in human nature, the divine right of some queens, freer will, the measurement of time as it has modified the concept of original sin, hydro-predestination, puritanism, and the medieval escape from perspective.

Since the age of twelve the authors of the I CHING, namely Fu Hsi, King Wên, the Duke of Chou, and Confucius, have been the light of my life—from them I have learned that the sage, the selfcontrolled man, dwells in actionless activity, poised between contraries.

Two years ago my father died. He had reached his sixtyfifth year when Joss, the Divine Being, called him to be numbered familiarly with his forebears.

This appears to Sappho in several ways an admirable biography. She wishes hers was as good. To be able to say, with such reticence, that her ancestors were great (tall) men—that, she confesses, she would love. Alas, like her, they were not high, though most of them believed, as she believes, that the stage is the best school of morality and the Church of Rome (some tricks of priestcraft excepted) certainly the true church.

Sappho's point, however, is only partly in the beauty of Chang's words. It should be considered that Chang enjoyed remarkable beauty of person. Consider it. He had faith, had Chang, in the needfulness of man's striving not to go mad. He could run backwards as fast as his father could run forwards. He could catch flies off the ceiling with his tongue. He believed that the proper use of prose was to describe description. He wore a Roman Style Toga Nightshirt. A child could sail across a lake in one of his shoes. The Count C, on the other hand, diligent and implausible, a true fellow of the pen, did not believe or disbelieve in one God. He had made his money out of a factory for embossing paper doilies. Everywhere he went, he opened bank accounts. His laughter was the thin snickering of a ghost. He walked like a priest, making a thrustaway kick with the side of his foot at each turn, as if to free his next step from the trammels of the soutane. He had the squint of a clerk and the stoop of a weasel. Have you never seen a weasel flow across the road in your headlights? His mind was bent.

Sappho does not know for certain whether Rossetti ever went to see Chang on any of his appearances in London. It might not have been unlike him to have done so; besides, the wretched appetite for horrors is present in us all (do not think that Sappho means to deny it in herself by making a statement like that).

Perhaps, though, the chairs were purchased for Rossetti by Howell? Howell did stand in relation to Rossetti, after all, as one who is a buyer of giant's chairs for a poet.

Sappho, who smells like a whore at a wake, would be overjoyed—if that is possible for one of her temperament, to be *over*joyed—she would, certainly, be joyed, deeply, yes, to the tips of her toes, if you would consider that characterisation a little carefully.

Mary Murder

MORE'S MOTHER'S MOTHER, his maternal grandmother, was Scotch. She was born in Egypt, a district of Glasgow, where her father, an architect, owned three houses of his own design : the first, a cottage on the Clyde, of severe dominant horizontal lines, influenced by traditional Japanese architecture perhaps; the second, a town house, in the shadow of St. Mungo's Cathedral, an agonisingly ornamented structure, crystallic, fussy, a frilly creamhorn composition in poured concrete; the third, an office in Buchanan Street, his most successful and unabashed contribution to the glory of the city, a snailshape insult, not unlike the main entrance hall to the museums of the Vatican, or the Guggenheim Museum, in New York City, designed by Frank Lloyd Wright. He was related by obscure descent to a niece of Jane Austen's. This niece had been one of the confidantes to whom the author talked from time to time about her work. Jane Austen had a need to know what her characters did after the end of their novels. She imparted some of these observations to her niece. They became a wellkept family secret. More's mother's mother's father, therefore, had the honour of being one of the few of his generation who knew that Captain Wentworth had squandered his fortune by backing a racing system that favoured the outsider in three-horse races, and repented, and turned into a woman. A true British Israelite, he also knew that the Faroes had to do with the Pharoahs, that King Arthur was a Philistine, and that Edinburgh and Jerusalem were the same place.[1] He was a

[1] For a thorough proof see Comyns Beaumont's BRITAIN—THE KEY TO WORLD HISTORY (London, 1949), especially Appendix C, page 259 (Old

78

man of the kind More most reveres and admires, below the middle size if anything and dressed habitually in black, his frockcoat buttoned to the throat where it met the sable stock. A silver wire was stretched across his teeth. His eyes were like prunes. He walked with a bobbing, springing motion which made him noticeable anywhere. He had laboured all his life to build a city to music just below the clouds. One flybutton was always left undone as a concession to the old phallic awareness, but he kept his eldest daughter on a strict rein.

Nevertheless, at the age of nineteen the girl managed to fall in love with a Frenchman from the Channel Islands. He was her senior by ten years, a fine figure of a fellow, variable in his spirits, boastful, given to crying into a cambric pocket handkerchief, an adroit and elegant flatterer, with shirt-collar *à la* Byron, his cheeks burning always as if from a slap, his hair parted in the middle, his clothes sour with sweat, impertinently

Edinburgh in its topography, its setting, the layout of its principal ancient streets, its wynds, its Castle rock, its former lakes or lochs, its Arthur's Seat, and its place-names offers a most complete comparison with ancient Jerusalem. Both were cities of great age—*Kaer Eden civitate antiquissima!*—both underwent fearful vicissitudes, both were praised for their matchless beauty, and both were the City of the Lion): and page 264, where the principal identifying landmarks are helpfully listed as follows:

JERUSALEM	EDINBURGH
David's City or Zion, or the Citadel	Edinburgh Castle
Millo	The Castle Moat
Mount Ophel and Upper City	Esplanade and Castle Hill
Upper Market Place	The Lawnmarket
Tyropoean Valley	George IV (North) Bridge
The Temple, Mt Moriah	St Giles' Cathedral and Law Courts (on the site of)
The High, Street of God	High Street
Lower Market Place and East Street	The Canongate
Third Hill 'over against' Acra	South Back of Canongate and Cowgate
Bezetha, New City	Calton Hill, and North Back of Canongate
Pool of Bethesda	Nor'Loch, now Princes St Station and beyond west

perfumed, absolutely French, pretty, petty, and puzzling. Not to make too many bones about it, she threw herself at him and was soon leading the knave a great dance in bed. She wrote to him too, cool stuff at first, such as, I wish I understood botany for your sake, as I might send you some specimens of moss, then it grew hotter, until she was writing him letters of an intensity of feeling and directness of expression which give the lie to the conventional imagination of the women of that age.

The Frenchman, for his part, poor chap, seems to have been moved to no more than physically obliging the girl out of the goodness of his heart. His face was handsome though rather outré; not a little like that of King Philip IV in the magnificent full-length portrait by Velasquez in the National Gallery, but superior in manliness, the expression of talent, and with hair which, being dark chestnut in tint, was free from the vapid effeminacy which marks the flaxen locks of Philip. He wore a Leghorn hat. His other main interest was in any possible social advantage the affair might bring him. Also, he hoped to improve his English from her letters.

His name was Emile. Emile Angel. He carried a richly-gilt memorandum-book. Whenever he looked at the sky he murmured God and whenever he saw a flower he said Mother.

Valley of Jehoshaphat	Princes St Gardens westwards
Pool of Siloam	South Loch or Old Borough Loch (now drained)
Fountain Gate	Bristo Port
King's Garden Gate	King's Bridge, foot of Castle
Gate of the Essenes	Canon Gate
Dung Gate	King's Stables Gate, or Dung Port
Valley Gate	West Port
Water Gate	Watergate, east end of City
Mount of Olives	King Arthur's Seat
Solomon's Palace of Lebanon and Gardens	Holyrood House (on site of) and Gardens
Joppa, the Port	Joppa, port of Edinburgh
Valley of Hinnom	Corstorphine Road
Mt Tophet, Place of Burning	Corstorphine Hill
Golgotha, Place of Skulls	Gogar's Mount and District
Hinnom	Falkirk

80

He wrote letters, as More does, mostly to himself. But Mary Murder, that was the girl, More's mother's mother, she was different. She wrote not to herself but to her cunt all on its little own in heaven.

Well, one day the Frenchman, Emile Angel, shivering in the very smile of summer, told the girl that he was turning over in his mind the possibility of leaving his ten-shillings-a-week job as a clerk in the employ of Huggins and Co. He said he kept thinking he heard a noise behind him, as if rats were at his heels. He wanted to emigrate to Portugal, where he might find better prospects of rising in the world. Alternatively, he would throw himself into the sewage disposal works. She, Mary Murder, was delicately panic-stricken by the plan.

She vowed she would go with him to Portugal, dressed as a cabinboy, in doublet and hose, and a red cap with a green feather.

He was not enthusiastic.

In fact to tell the truth he seems to have been using the prospect of Portugal as a threat. He wanted Mary to marry him, to be kind about his stammer, to cure him of his mental deafness, to take him rides in her green barouche, to share the fruits of her cryptaesthesia with him, to tell her father his opinion of Victor Hugo, to give him poppyseeds to make him giddy, and money, and kisses elsewhere than on the buttocks, and a start, as you might say, in life. He had ambitions to be a surveyor. He was fed up with being an outside passenger on the omnibuses. His present position gave him a pain. He was, after all, an interloper, an outsider, a survivor of the Revolution of 1848, no more than her puppet, her plaything, her quencher (to the best of his ability). Being masterful, he resented this.

Mary, forced to choose between father and lover, knew that she had everything to lose by loyalty. She made a few tentative and halfhearted attempts to discover her father's atti-

tude towards RUY BLAS, then she retreated, writing to Angel:
A long last lingering fond farewell, alas, my duck, for I have
given my male parent my word of honour that I shall never
more communicate with you. The sun is setting on the Crans-
ton Hill Water Company. I am weeping, pet, the smudgy
marks on the paper are my tears. You will never get one who
will love you as I have done. It almost breaks my heart to
return to you your likeness and chain, but I must not keep
them. It is night, night. Write me a parting sonnet, darling
of my soul, the last word I shall ever receive from you in
this life. Let it be in the Petrarchan form, the other offends my
ears with its epigrammatic clinching harshness in the final
couplet, altogether too pat. It is true, dear good little husband
mine, that Surrey and Miss Anne Whateley managed well
enough with their ABAB CDCD EFEF GG, yet old ways are best
ways, and to my nerves there is a sublimer, more steeped
beauty in the Dantean or Petrarchan ABBA ABBA CDE CDE.
Incidentally, my all, I think you know me well enough to
realise that I will permit of some small variation in the sestet,
if music or meaning demands it. Thus, beloved, if you want
ABBA ABBA CDC DCD, I shall not object. In that case I suggest
the following rhymes might be at once tasteful, euphonious,
and sensibly malleable:

> *despair*
> *shrine*
> *divine*
> *air*
> *wear*
> *mine*
> *thine*
> *bare*
> *lust*
> *consume*
> *dust*
> *womb*
> *thrust*

82

tomb (if you consider *womb/tomb* vulgar, my only, only
love, my pet, my hen, my best of men, then you could
try *room, loom, groom, gloom, doom, whom, broom,*
or even at a pinch, *boom*)
or, dear heart, supposing you prefer it ABBA ABBA CDD CCD
then I recommend :
peep
strong
thong
weep
asleep
gong
long
deep
rain
task
mask
again
pain
ask
or, if you go for ABBA ABBA CDDC EE (which is the uttermost
I can grant in the way of permissiveness, love, the sestet already
beginning that dreadful middle-class swoon towards the couplet) then you might try :
years
luck
stuck
tears
fears
suck
duck
disappears
lay
knows
flows
day

thee (or *Thee*)

memory.

I do hope, my sweet, that one of these suggestions will prove an inspiration to your muse. In addition to the sonnet, if you will, I should enjoy a limerick, on these undermentioned rhymes:

chaste

taste

love

above

waste (or *waist*)

the subject of the limerick to be selected from the following:

(*a*) Queen Joan, barefoot and dishevelled, finding sanctuary in a church dedicated to the Virgin, during the Naples earthquake at the time of Petrarch's stay there

(*b*) That God, whom we suppose to be personal, is not simply the world

(*c*) The loveshaped Combination Room at St John's College, Cambridge

(*d*) Blue.

As a final favour I ask that you burn all my letters the day you receive this. A kiss, my pet. A dear, tender, sweet, kind, loving embrace. Adieu, my much beloved, my dear dear Emile. God bless you, make you happy. Adieu. Good night. The stars are shining above the sourmilk carts on Rutherglen Bridge. I wish I were with you, I would be happier than I am. Again farewell, with much, much love, and warm loving kisses. That bridge used to be a deathtrap, but the municipality, with praiseworthy spirit, has rendered it safe and commodious now. I am, with much love, for ever your own dear sweet little pet wife, but like Lady Godiva must now come to my clo'es. All the best, Mary. PS: you may, if you wish, annotate my letters before burning.

Angel was a cool creature. More is not at all inclined to say that from first to last his conduct was that of a man of honour.

He had no intention of writing sonnets. Even less, of burning Mary's letters.

Look at it from his point of view for a moment, and you will understand why. A man holding a respectable job, known as a responsible character, wearing a dark brownish coat and a Balmoral bonnet, liked by all those who came in contact with him, spoken of in the highest possible terms by the three landladies with whom he had lodged, he had been employed to slake the needs of this summerblooded girl and was now to be discarded, his usefulness spent. Not only that, but he was instructed to write the parting sonnet to their affair. What indignity! His Gallicism boiled in his tepid heart. He found a way to resume their trysts, and by eating cocklebread he managed to keep his end up, but now a new resentment ached in him and gave him no peace: he was looking for a chance to humiliate Mary Murder because her sexual patronage humiliated him.

Mary, not to be daunted, crossed her legs behind his back and even began to dream of marriage, going to her mother and getting her face slapped for her trouble. She wrote, then, to Angel: I was told by Mama that she was sure Papa would sooner see me in my grave than, jockey mine, your wife . . . I was told that you were poor and but a clerk who frittered his time away . . . I was told that I should look higher (than the waist I suppose!) . . . The old faggot told me I should never never be your wife with their consent and blessing. My love for you, she said, was a sin against herself and my father, and also God. I said that I intended to marry you, and that nothing would change my resolve. She said that she was ashamed to hear me say such things. I said, But he is a good Catholic. She said, Man does not live by bread alone.

Angel replied with ladykilling evasiveness. He did not want to marry Mary unless there was money in it that would raise him up and drag her down. He knew that if he married her and forced her to live in poverty with him she would find opportunities to humiliate him further, for there is nothing that humiliates a man more than trying to make his wife live on *his* level.

Mary, sensitive to her beau's reluctance, was pleased when her father introduced a new agent into the plot. This was a merchant called Mr Minnow, a partner of the firm of John Houldsworth and Co., a rich, safe, probable man, with a belly like a swing. He wore a rusty black frockcoat and went for his holidays to Morar, where he walked the white beaches that were to his eye the colour of oatmeal porridge with sugar on it, the sea his milk each morning. One day when the sun was hot he undid two buttons of his waistcoat and went for a frisky paddle. He was an outdoor type, devoted to his owls and his chameleons and his dog called Love. It was Mr Minnow's proud boast that he had never smoked a manufactured cigarette. He proceeded to roll one now, tucking in the stray ends of tobacco with the point of a cedarwood pencil.

That done, he proposed holy matrimony to Mary Murder.

The girl was shrewd enough to be flattered, and accepted.

A problem arose: how was Mary to get her letters back from Angel? She saw him in a fresh light, and realised that he might blackmail her. She wrote to him lyrically, on paper smelling of marl and jasmine, not mentioning Mr Minnow, asking him to return her letters, as there was autumn on both sides. Angel did not answer. Mary, losing her nerve, wrote again: Emile! Write no more! Neither to Papa, nor to *any other*! On Wednesday night, the feast of Saints Saturninus, Dativus, and others, martyrs of Africa, I shall open my shutter and then you shall come to the area gate. I shall see you. We shall talk. Oh, Emile be not harsh to me. I am the most guilty miserable wretch on the face of the earth. Emile, do not drive me to death. When I ceased to love you, believe me, it was not to love another. I am free from all engagements at present. Emile, for God's sake, do not send my letters to Papa!

Lies, you might tut. And you would be right, of course.

Mary was engaged to Mr Minnow, and already knew him well enough to know that he slept very soundly with one eye open. But, even more pernicious than that, notice the shalls. Angel noticed them, and did not reply, keeping this letter in the same drawer where he had her others.

Mary Murder was not used to silence answering her when she spoke.

She decided that she probably hated Emile Angel.

She waited until the feast of Saints Saturninus, Dativus, and others, was passed, then, when it became plain that the treacherous Frenchman had no intention of either replying, or coming to her call, or returning the letters she had written him at the height of her infatuation, she sent her maid to Whangie the chemist to buy a small phial of prussic acid.

Whangie would not give prussic acid to one so young. When the maid came back and told Mary this, Mary smiled. Shit, she said. The sound of her laughter was like the clinking of chandeliers in a white and gold room where soldiers have flung open the doors.

She altered her tactics. She wrote softly again to Angel, to open up all the old wounds with dainty fingers. Her motive was to kill him with bewilderments. She had made up some of her heart to marry Mr Minnow. She wanted to finish with the nuisance from Jersey in one way or another.

On a showery Monday morning, Mary Murder bought arsenic, sixpennyworth, from a druggist in Sauchiehall Street. She said she was troubled by rats. She told the chemist that was why she needed the arsenic. The chemist told her that he was not fond of selling arsenic for getting rid of rats, because it was so dangerous. He recommended phosphorus paste, which he said would do as well. She told him that she had used it, but it had failed. She got the arsenic. It was mixed with soot.

On Thursday of that week, Emile Angel was taken ill. At about the same time he started to pronounce his name Englishly, which was not much admired or appreciated by the

87

Glaswegians. His landlady, Anne Duthie or Jenkins, knocking on his door about eight in the morning, got no answer. She knocked again. He said, Come in. She went in. He was in bed. He said, I have been very unwell, look what I have vomited. She said, I think that's bile. It was a greenish substance like gruel. There was a great deal of it. She said, Why did you not call me? He said, Coming home I got this fury in my bowels and stomach. When I was taking off my clothes I lay down on the floor. I thought I was going to die, and that only God would see me. I was not able to ring the bell. He asked her to make him a little tea, and said he thought he would not go out. She emptied what he had vomited. She advised him to go to a doctor, and he said he would. This illness made a great change in his appearance. He looked yellow and dull, became dark under the eyes, and the red in his cheeks was more broken. It cannot be proved that Angel had been with Mary the night before.

Mary trotted along to another chemist, wearing her russet gown, with another bright sixpence, and asked for more arsenic, again mentioning rats. This chemist also suggested phosphorus paste. She said she had got arsenic before. He said he would rather give her something else. She said she did not insist on arsenic, but that she would prefer it. He said that he never sold arsenic to anyone without entering it in a book, and that she must sign her name, and write down what she was going to use it for. She said she did not mind doing that. She got an ounce, mixed with indigo. There was a further flurry of letters between her and the Frenchman. He was wary.

Yet on Sunday the 22nd of February, 1857, he was taken ill again, calling Anne Duthie or Jenkins to him at four on the Monday morning to show her that he had vomited the same kind of stuff as before, in colour and otherwise, and complaining of the same pain in his bowels and stomach, and of thirst. He was very cold. She put more clothes on him, and jars of hot water to his feet and stomach. She made some

88

tea, he had a great many drinks, toast and water and lemon and water. He did not rise in the forenoon. He got a little better. He was away from his office for eight days.

No rat corpses were to be seen.

A week later, Mary bought more arsenic. She boasted in the chemist's of the number she had killed with the last lot.

The number of what? asked the apothecary's apprentice, a Mr Rose MacGregor, busy with his plasters, pills, and ointment boxes.

Rats, said Mary Murder.

Slippery blisses, twinkling eyes, soft completion of faces, and smooth excess of hands, murmured Mr Rose MacGregor.

It was later proved that this was entirely untrue.

Mary now wrote to Angel more hotly than ever, a letter in an envelope posted at Glasgow, General Office or pillarbox, on the 21st of March, 1857, between 9 a.m. and halfpast 12 p.m. if pillarbox, and if General Office between 11.45 a.m. and 1 p.m., and deliverable in any case between 1.30 and 3 that same afternoon. She asked him to come and see her: Why, my beloved, did you not come to me? My God! My food! Are you ill? Come to me, sweet one. I waited and waited for you but you came not. I shall wait again tomorrow night same hour and arrangement. Do come, sweet love, my own dear love of a sweetheart. It is the day of St Lea, widow, of Rome. Come sweetness, and clasp me to your heart. Come, and we shall be happy on the peaks of the wandering moon. A kiss, a kiss, fond love, adieu, with tender embraces ever believe me to be your own ever dear fond sugar Mary xxx.

The Frenchman came again on Sunday, bringing her twelve new marabout feathers. Or did he?

Perhaps he came again, but brought her a very fine real white Brussels lace Marie Antoinette fichu.

Perhaps he came again but brought her no gifts.

Perhaps he did not come again at all.

Perhaps he replied by sending her a parcel of calves' testicles and two pieces of useless advice.

Perhaps he consulted his friend Louis Parsenell.

Perhaps Louis Parsenell was not his friend.

Perhaps Louis Parsenell was a bit of bad handwriting saying Love's Farewell.

The facts in the case are these: Angel had been away for a few days, at Bridge of Allan, a police burgh with a pumproom on the lefthand tributary of the Forth. On Sunday, the 22nd of March, on receipt of a forwarded letter, he hurried back to Glasgow, foregoing the pleasures of the hydropathic building and the Macfarlane museum of fine art and natural history. He left his lodgings about nine. Before he went out he said to Anne Duthie or Jenkins, Please give me the passkey, I am not sure but I may be late. She saw him next about halfpast two on the Monday morning. He did not use the passkey. The bell rang with great violence. She rose. Who's there? she called. He said, It is I, Mrs Jenkins, open the door, if you please. She did so. He was standing with his arms closed across his stomach. He said, I am very bad. I am going to have another vomiting of that bile. He said he had thought he would never get home, he was so bad on the road. After he came in he asked for a little water. She filled a tumbler. He drank it empty. He asked for tea. She went into the room before he was half undressed. He was vomiting severely. It was the same kind of matter as before. There was gaslight, so she could see it clearly enough. She said, Have you been taking something that disagrees with you? referring to his food at Bridge of Allan. He said, No, I was never better than I was at the coast, meaning, as she understood, at Bridge of Allan. She said, You have not taken enough medicine though, and he said, I never approved of medicine. He was chilly and cold, wishing hot water to his feet and stomach. She got him jars of hot water, also three pairs of railway blankets and two mats. He grew a little easier. He became very bad at four. She said she would go for Dr Elbë in Dundas Street. He thanked her, but said it was too much trouble so early. She said it was no trouble. He said he feared she would not find

90

the way. She said, No fear. He got a little better, about five he got very bad again, his bowels got very bad. She said she would go to the nearest doctor, a Dr Gleneden. He asked what kind of a doctor he was. She said a good doctor. He told her to go and bring him. She went for Dr Gleneden. Dr Gleneden could not come. He said to give twentyfive drops of laudanum, and to put a mustard blister on the stomach and hot water. She went back. Angel said he could not take laudanum. She gave him plenty of hot water. He said that a blister would be no use, he was only retching. About seven he was dark about the eyes. She said she would go again for Dr Gleneden. He was anxious that she should. When Dr Gleneden came he ordered mustard. She left the room to get it. She did not hear the doctor ask Angel what was wrong. She said to the doctor, Look what he has vomited. The doctor said, Take it away, it is making him faintish. She got mustard. The doctor put it on. He said he would wait to see the effect. He gave him morphia. He stayed about half an hour. Anne Duthie or Jenkins went in with more hot water. When she was applying it Angel said, Oh, Mrs Jenkins, this is the worst attack I ever had. He said, I feel something here. He pointed to his forehead. Dr Gleneden said, It must be something internally. I can see nothing wrong. Angel said, Can you do anything, doctor? Doctor Gleneden said time and quietness were required. Anne Duthie or Jenkins left the room. She pointed to the doctor to come. When they were outside she asked him what was wrong. Dr Gleneden asked if Angel was a person that tippled. She said he was not. The doctor said he was like a man that tippled. She assured him Angel was not given to drink. She said, It is strange, this is the second time he has gone out well and returned very ill. I must speak to him and ask the cause. The doctor said, That will be an after-explanation. He promised he would be back between ten and eleven. The first time she went back to him Angel asked her what the doctor thought. She replied, He thinks you will get over it. To which he said, I am far worse than the doctor thinks. She saw him several times. He always said, If I could get some sleep, I should be better. About nine she drew the curtains. He looked badly. She went out and in three or four times. The last time she went in he said, Oh, if I could get five minutes' sleep, I think I would get better. These were his last words. She left him. She went back quietly in ten minutes. She thought he was asleep. She went out. The doctor came soon after. He asked for his patient. She said he was newly asleep, it was a pity to waken him. He said he would like to see him. They went in. Dr Gleneden felt Angel's pulse. He lifted up his head. It fell down. He told her Angel was dead.

Dr Gleneden went away down the cobbled street, the wind shrugging in his cape.

A postmortem examination was made. It established that Angel had died as the result of poisoning. The incision made on opening the belly and chest revealed a considerable deposit of subcutaneous fat. The heart appeared large for the individual, but not so large, in the doctor's opinion, as to mean disease. Its surfaces presented, externally, some opaque patches, such as are frequently seen on this organ without giving rise to any symptoms. Its right cavities were filled with dark fluid blood. The lungs, the liver, and the spleen appeared quite healthy. The gall bladder was moderately full of bile, but contained no calculi. The stomach and intestines, externally, presented nothing abnormal. The stomach, being tied at both ends, was removed from the body. Its contents, consisting of about half a pint of dark fluid resembling cocoa, were poured into a clear bottle, and the organ itself was laid open along its great curvature. The mucous membrane, except for a slight extent at the lesser curvature, was then seen to be deeply injected with blood, presenting an appearance of dark red mottling, and its substance was remarked to be soft, being easily torn by scratching with the fingernail. The body was then coffined, and the coffin laid in a vault at the Ramshorn

92

Church. Seven days later a further inspection was carried out. Angel presented much the same appearance generally as when the doctors had left him. They remarked, however, that the features had lost their former pinched look, and that the general surface of the skin, instead of the tawny or dingy hue it had worn before, had become rather florid. All agreed that the evidences of putrefaction were much less marked than they usually are at such a date—the ninth day after death and the fifth after burial. The duodenum, along with the upper part of the small intestine, consisting of part of the descending colon and sigmoid flexure, along with a portion of the rectum, after using the precaution of placing ligatures at both ends of the bowel, was removed and placed in a clean jar. A portion of the liver, being about a sixth, was cut off and placed in another clean jar. They then opened the head in the usual manner, and observed nothing calling for remark beyond a greater degree of vascularity of the membranes of the brain than is ordinary. A portion of the brain was removed and placed in a third clean jar. The doctors than adjourned, taking the vessels with them. The duodenum and portion of small intestine were found to measure together 36 inches in length. Their contents, poured into a glass measure, were found to amount to four fluid ounces, and to consist of a turbid, sanguinolent fluid, having suspended in it much flocculent matter, which settled towards the bottom, whilst a few mucouslike masses floated on the surface. The mucous membrane of this part of the bowels was then examined. Its colour was decidedly redder than natural, and this redness was more marked over several patches, portions of which, under close scrutiny, were found to be eroded. A few small ulcers, about a sixteenth of an inch in diameter, and having elevated edges, were observed at the upper part of the duodenum.

Angel's body was also measured at this time. His vital statistics were as follows :

Height	...	...	...	...	78 inches
Circumference of head		...	...	24 inches
Round the chest	...	...	...	48 inches
Across the shoulders		...	...	24 inches
Length of arm (humerus)	...		...	16 inches
Length of forearm (radius)			...	24 inches
Circumference of forearm	...		...	12 inches
Length of middle finger		...	...	4 inches
Diameter of hand	...	...	...	6 inches
Length of thighbone (femur)		...	24 inches
Length of legbone (tibia)	...		...	18 inches
Length of foot	...	...	...	12 inches
Diameter of foot	...	...	...	6 inches

It is perhaps worth noting that these figures do not contain a single odd number.

Now Angel's ambitions had taken him into some of the more elaborate reaches of society. He had lit fireworks with Monsieur August Vauvert de Mean, the French Consul in Glasgow, a man of consummate fashion, whose very bootblacking was said to be made from champagne. De Mean, given the task of going through the dead man's effects, came across Mary's letters. His gorge rose. He took a cab to her house and waved them under her breasts, demanding the truth.

The truth? said Mary. What is the truth? I loved him.

Are you a silent Protestant? asked de Mean.

No! said Mary. I have my pride—and prejudices.

The Consul preferred not to believe her. He put the question again in different ways. Mary went on turning the handle of her lockstitch sewing machine. Her plump white arm with its gold bracelet shone in the gaslight. Her hair threw a soft shadow on her forehead. Her eyes watched the material flowing away below the needle. Her seam was running crooked. She snapped the thread and stood up. Monsieur Mean, she said, I swear to you that I have not seen Angel for three whole weeks.

De Mean asked why, though, she had continued writing to Angel after she had become engaged to Mr Minnow. Mary said that it was because she wanted her earlier letters back, because they were indiscreet and she would rather they were destroyed; alternatively, if they were to be published she wished to have them properly edited.

Mary was arrested that darkfall and charged with the murder of Emile Angel.

The trial began by candlelight during a thunderstorm.

The general opinion was that she was guilty, but beautiful, her neck in particular milky white, with lovely little lavender veins showing here and there, like the guiding lines she had used sometimes when she wrote to Angel, showing faintly through the thick white notepaper.

She told the court in a distinct and unshaken tone, her manner calm, her gaze candid, that she had bought the arsenic to make cakes for the rats, and to use in washing her feet because it was good for the complexion. On the night of the murder, she said, she had been to the opera. They were doing LUCREZIA BORGIA. She enjoyed it. She never drank cocoa.

Mr Rose MacGregor's evidence was decisive. Love without return, he said, is like an answer without a question.

The jury brought in their verdict Scottishly: *Not Proven*.

There was singing in court.

Mary went free.

She wore a grebe muff and round collarette.

She lived unobtrusively for the rest of her life, becoming a Socialist and marrying twice. The first husband was an artist called George Wardle, a friend of William and Jane Morris. Bernard Shaw met her and commented: One day Belfort Bax rushed in to tell me that Mrs Wardle was Mary Murder and we should all be poisoned.

They were not.

Shaw added : She seemed an ordinary goodhumoured woman with nothing sinister about her. But then Shaw's ignorance of women was such that he thought Joan of Arc was not a witch.

When Wardle died, Mary went to America, and married again, More's grandfather.

Now to the not-bad-picture-whose-subject-was-too-dreadful. Perhaps you have guessed? The woman whom Treffry Dunn described as all forlorn in an oar-and-rudderless boat, with its sail flapping in the wind about her, alone on a wide and weary waste of water, that was Mary. After she married Wardle and came to London (where Wardle was manager of Morris's culture factory) she was wellknown to Rossetti. The picture was but one of his several interpretations of her tragedy. It is the sort of picture which needs, as critical comment, only a restatement of its subject :

Not Proven.

Perhaps, though, a little mild explication might be in order. The blazing city behind the boat was not Troy, but Glasgow, the Glasgow Mary had fled after her trial, because there were so many then to flood her with sonnets. As for the dragons and demons and sea-monsters that beset her round, perhaps they were figments of her puritanic fear, or of Rossetti's Italianite imagination of that fear. Perhaps they were real presences to her, attendants on her, Furies. More does not know. He has no family secret that he can reveal to you, as to whether Mary was guilty or not of the murder of her poor lover. For what it is worth, More thinks she was innocent. She was beautiful. She did not marry Mr Minnow. She must have known that if she murdered Emile Angel she was running risk of her letters coming to light in the most unsuitable literary atmosphere.

96

The Wandering Jew

WE CAME TO AMSTERDAM in the company of Captain Rufus
Coate, of whom we have already spoken. Of the city itself
we remember little. Description is no part of our design. Say
the word Amsterdam to us and we think not of sunlight
falling in a colonnade, or a white armada of swans going under
a yellow bridge, or dim roofs in the rain, or smoke from
marble chimneys, or any of that nonsense. Rather our minds
turn to images of the bourse, of bullion and munitions and
shipbuilding. Amsterdam : Burlamachi and Calandrini financ-
ing Buckingham's illstarred campaigns with giant loans for
which the Duke's jewels, and some of the Crown jewels, were
held in security. Amsterdam : was not Burlamachi amongst
those merchant strangers tried in 1619 on a charge of having
exported coin? (He was himself deep in debt to Calandrini
when he failed in 1633.) Amsterdam : in 1642, the Crown
jewels again in Dutch hands . . . Queen Henrietta Maria,
that much misunderstood one, travelling thence to put them in
pawn for funds for the royalist cause. Amsterdam : the Portuguese Jews that came in the early seventeenth century, their
bright and buckled shoes. Amsterdam : the French envoy,
Buzanval, observing the haste with which the Dutch set off to
the East, the sleepers still in their eyes, to prise open the
frigid pearl of the Orient, hitherto in Spanish hands. Thus
our bibliography of a mind ticks over at the drop of the word
Amsterdam. Forgive us, for we wasted our leaves in the libra-
ries of Europe.

It was in Amsterdam that we met the Wandering Jew.
There had been a hurricane visiting Holland in the days before

we docked. When we set foot ashore we were handed a sealed packet wrapped in oilskin, by one whom we recognised as having been sometime in the employ of our stepfather, the Count C. The packet contained an unsigned message in our mother's handwriting, advising us to proceed with discretion to a certain café, not far from the waterfront. We did so. The name of this café, translated, was *The Goat and Compasses*. There, obeying instructions, we seated ourselves at a table within view of the door and opened the copy of Percy's RELIQUES OF ANCIENT BRITISH POETRY which we carried everywhere with us in those days. Our mother's note, with all the usual flourishes and underlinings that signified nothing, had told us to position our person thus, and open our book at page 116. She was aware that we had the 1906 Dent Everyman edition, in two volumes.

We opened the first volume at the advised page and found it contained some idle discussion of a ballad of Robin Hood and Guy of Gisborne. None of this was of much interest, save a reference to Stukeley's PALAOGRAPHIA BRITANNICA II, 1746, which gave a pedigree of Hood, proving that he had solid pretensions to the earldom of Huntingdon, and that his true name was Robert Fitzooth. We puzzled over this. Our mother was aware that we had been familiar with Stukeley on Hood from about the age of seven. The name Fitzooth had even been introduced into The Game. Why, then, should she bother to direct us to sit in a café in Amsterdam reading a page of notes that we knew more or less backwards, and which appeared of small significance in any case?

Then we realised that she must have meant page 116 in the *second* volume of the Dent Everyman edition, though a quick check of her note assured us that she had not said this in so many words. We turned to page 116 in the second volume (which we carried in our left pocket for convenience) and found that it contained one brief stanza, spoken by Ignorance in the Somersetshire dialect in a ballad called PLAIN TRUTH AND BLIND IGNORANCE. We read this minutely, looking for symbols. It seemed to have little for us, though the last four lines had a pleasing ambiguity :

> *Believing in the Gospel,*
> *And passion of his Zon,*
> *And with the zubtil papistes*
> *Ich have for ever done.*

When we looked below this on the page, we read as follows :

III. *The Wandering Jew.* The story of the Wandering Jew is of considerable antiquity. It had obtained full credit in this part of the world before the year 1228, as we learn from Matthew Paris, for in that year it seems there came an Armenian archbishop into England, to visit the shrines and reliques preserved in our churches, who being entertained at the monastery of St Albans, was asked several questions relating to his country, &c. Among the rest a monk, who sat near him, inquired if he had ever seen or heard of the famous person named Joseph, that was so much talked of, who was present at our Lord's crucifixion and conversed with him, and who was still alive in confirmation of the Christian faith. The archbishop answered that the fact was true. And afterwards one of his train, who was wellknown to a servant of the abbot's, interpreting his master's words, told them in French that his lord knew the person they spoke of very well, that he had dined at his table but a little while before he left the east, that he had been Pontius Pilate's porter, by name Cartaphilus, who, when they were dragging Jesus out of the door of the Judgment-hall, struck him with his fist on the back, saying, Go faster, Jesus, go faster! Why dost thou linger? Upon which Jesus looked at him with a frown, and said, I indeed am going, but though shalt tarry till I come. Soon after he was converted, and baptized by the name of Joseph. He lives for ever, but at the end of every hundred years falls into an incurable illness, and at length into a fit or ecstasy, out of

99

which when he recovers, he returns to the same state of youth he was in when Jesus suffered, being then about thirty years of age. He remembers all the circumstances of the death and resurrection of Christ, the saints that arose with him, the composing of the apostles' creed, their preaching, and dispersion, and is himself a very grave and holy person. This is the substance of Matthew Paris's account, who was himself a monk of St Albans, and was living at the time when this Armenian archbishop made the above relation. Since his time several imposters have appeared at intervals under the name and character of the Wandering Jew; whose several histories may be seen in Calmet's DICTIONARY OF THE BIBLE. See also the TURKISH SPY, vol. ii, book 3, let I. The story that is copied in the following ballad is of one who appeared in Hamburg in 1547, and pretended he had been a Jewish shoemaker at the time of Christ's crucifixion. The ballad, however, seems to be of later date. It is preserved in black letter in the Pepys collection.

We read the ballad, sitting with pins-and-needles in our left leg at that café table in Amsterdam, and believe us our sensibilities were rawly rasped by the tedious doggerel of the thing. Now it no longer moves or affects us one way or the other.

We had barely set the book down on the table (it had been necessary to hold it near our eyes, for the light within the café was not good) when the door opened and a man came in. He was tall, haggard, confidently camp in manner. His hair was long, protruding from beneath a green felt hat and hanging down at the back almost to his shoulders. It was brown and curly, mixed with grey, and floated around his collar like a mane. There was so much powder in the wrinkles on his cheeks that he looked like a peeling wall in a thunderstorm. He had no shoes on. It had begun to rain outside. The swinging of the door brought a sweet sharp stink of rain and reawakened dust into the café. The proprietor stood staring out without pleasure at the rain and the dusk together, then he moved smiling to light candles on the wet tabletops. We ordered two cups of cocoa.

The newcomer looked about him for a moment. His eyes rested glowingly on us. He shook off the grim cape he wore round his shoulders. It was hard not to laugh, for we saw that the lower half of his body was strangely clad, a pair of sailor's trousers splayed out where they met his bare feet, over these he wore a sort of priest's frockcoat reaching to the knees. A bag of Transvaal tobacco swung from his belt. From his gait it was easy to deduce that he had a seaman's mistrust of land.

He strode across and sat down at our table without any word of introduction, taking off his hat and lighting a cigarette. He smoked in that kind of furious sucking way which is characteristic of great smokers. Much smoking, however, had not dried up his skin to the consistence of blotting paper and to the colour of tobacco ash as it does in some cases, but tobacco juice, which seemed to ooze from his face like perspiration, or rather like oil, had made his complexion of a yellow green colour, something like vegetable marrow. Although his face was as hairless as a woman's, there was not a feature in it that was not masculine. His cheekbones were high and his jaw was of the mould which we so often associate with the prizefighter, yet he looked as if he might somehow be a gentleman. We waited patiently until he had translated half his cigarette into smoke. Then he began to speak in a clear, low, unhurried, but gratingly weary voice.

Friend, he said, I fear one thing only—the second coming. Get me? That I fear because at Christ's first penetration of time and flesh I chanced to make him angry. On that second penetration, in the last day, he might again prove to have set his heart against me. Then what shall become of me? I live for death only. If Christ is angry when he comes again, if he even has toothache, or indigestion, or feels generally out of sorts,

101

he may not kill me. O my brother, think of that . . . To live another lifetime of Christianity were too much.

We asked him, conversationally: What was the Crucifixion like?

He said it was good at the time but had been overrated since. Then he wiped his hands as though he was washing them, and manufactured a grin. It was a capricious grin, but not unpleasant. His lips were gross and wet, a flautist's.

We asked him what he had been doing since Matthew Paris wrote that account of the Armenian knowledge of him in 1228. He said he had wandered wondering about the world, looking at other things with the monocle through which he had seen God.

Wait! we cried, remembering. We seem to call to mind some account of your appearance in Germany. Is that right? About the middle of the sixteenth century? You were going under the romantic name of Ahasuerus. Wasn't it a drunken bishop who saw you?

I can't abide a bishop, he said. The occasion was during the nasty winter of 1542, when I came in out of the snow with a pregnant nun to listen to a sermon at Hamburg. I remember the text for that sermon. Matthew xv., 32 : I have compassion on the multitude . . . for they have nothing to eat. The bishop was so pissed he said Matthew meant spiritual food! I could have strangled him with my bare feet!

The details of all this were set down in a letter, we told him, dated the 29th of June, 1564, and afterwards printed in good German and tolerable French. Your own language was said to be German, in the dialect of Saxony.

That's right, he said. I am usually polite.

Yet when you appeared in the Netherlands in 1575, we said, you were spouting Spanish.

I was still being polite then, he said. Besides, he added, there is only one language I prefer to Spanish.

We did not think then that we might ask him what that language was. It seemed altogether too wide and vulgar a sweaty opening to be taken advantage of. We had a feeling, also, that he was deliberately teasing us and would not have told us which language even had we taken our sensibility to pieces and our courage in both lapels then and there and asked him.

We said, Then you were in the West Indies?

Alas, yes, he said. I was walking. It was hot. I met a woman leaning on a white gate. Hello, she said. Hello, I said. What's your job? she said. I'm a poet, I said. Well, said she, you've a rare day for it!

And France? we said.

I came to France in 1604, he said, having won fortunes at roulette in Salamanca, Venice, and Naples.

We have read of it, we said. There were hurricanes.

There are always hurricanes, said the Jew. He opened his mouth as if to laugh, but there was no laugh. We saw that his throat had forgotten laughter. His teeth were like gravestones. In Brittany and Picardy even now, he went on, the peasants make the sign of the cross against the hurricanes and swear, C'est le Juif-errant qui passe! They have a fetching little ballad, you know, which begins:

Est-il rien sur la terre
  Qui soit plus suprenant
Que la grande misère
  Du pauvre Juif-errant?
Qui son sort malheureux
  Paraît triste et fâcheux!

His French accent was impeccable, without the least trace of a *patois*. One might have sworn he had been born in the better part of Beauvais.

We asked him if it was true that he had once been heavyweight boxing champion of the world.

He admitted that he had.

And Beethoven? we said.

103

He confessed that he had been Beethoven, and made a gesture like a man whose stilts have caught fire, as if to dismiss the incident.

His voice blushed. Never mind that, he said, never mind, only if you had invalid parents to maintain in Portugal . . .

We asked him, What is your name now?

Isaac Laquedem, he said. These words were trolled out with a seductive soupçon of a foreign accent, raising his eyebrows as though that was an end of the matter.

And then, without more ado, he began to speak again in a low, rattling tone, as though he had springs clicking and whirring in his throat, his face a smooth moon and his eyes shining as he told of a strange dream he had dreamt the night before, a niagara of lies. In the dream he had been reading a dictionary full of droll definitions. Under TRUTH, for example, it said *kindness*, under BEAUTY it said *that which imitates the perfect*, under ART it said *a dream of the actual*, under MAN it said *see Woman*, under WOMAN it said *mattress*, under MEMORY it said *a mild attack of truth*, under PERSONALITY it said *moss*, under RELIGION it said *a way to think the world is round instead of round about*, under LOGIC it said *what we think we think when we think we are*, under NATURE it said *nothingness turned inside out*, under MUSIC it said *energy in love with its own tail*, and so on, and so on, all quite nonsense.

Now let us say at once that we did not believe this person was really the Wandering Jew. We do not mean that we had crude doubts of the sort that might occur at such a juncture to an atheistical mind. We had no objection to the idea of the Wandering Jew. We were prepared to believe in the idea, but we were not able to credit this manifestation of it as being adequate. We found him irrefutable but unacceptable. That is to say: We suspected that the man was a phoney.

The light seemed to be melting into darkness. The café grew more and more murky. Our companion's hair was already

104

part of the dark around it, it was impossible to tell where gloom ended and he began. Only his eyes were sudden and distinct, staring into ours. They looked like pools of poison.

He said, Brother, you do not believe in me.

We protested.

You do not believe in me, he said. Yet I love you.

We fell silent.

He had shut one of his eyes and looked at us with the other. It seemed filmed with pain. We experienced an odd need to shut one of our own eyes, as if this would help him. We had to fight this impulse before we mastered it.

You are doubting my part in the story, he said, without reproach. Yet my story is your story. You know that. So you are doubting a part of yourself. You do not believe in yourself. Yet I love you.

His voice was still immediate. But his body seemed to be dwindling, rotting, collapsing into dusk. As for his face, he would soon have none, for it was melting fast, like wax in a flame.

Brother! we cried.

Murderer, he said softly. And then: Have you never, shaving yourself with an ordinary razor, had the thought how easy it would be to end existence by drawing the edge of the razor through the important structures in the neck?

We reached across the table with shaking hands. There was no one there.

The café proprietor came and set down a stout yellow candle in a blue saucer before us. In this country cocoa is very thin, he said. In France chocolate is as thick as porridge. He walked away as if trying not to spill himself.

The Amsterdam affair demanded that we change our life. We changed it. All at once certain things that had troubled us—the words Pascal wrote on a scrap of paper and which were found sewn up in his doublet after his death, Nicholas of Cusa's statement that God is to be found beyond the coincidence of contradictories, certain opaque passages in Ruysbroeck—these fell into place. We no longer cared whether we lived or died, whether we knew or did not know ourself. Consequently we lived. Accordingly we knew.

Mr Benjamin

WHEN HIS Uncle Julius died, leaving him a soothing tract of freehold and a good round sum at his bankers, Doctor Copper was suddenly a rich man. Riches did not take him by surprise. All his life he had been moneyed in imagination, and borne himself as though he slept in silk and had thirty-three thousand pounds judiciously invested by advisers who telephoned once a month to report on new advances in his fortune—nothing spectacular, just a steady jubilation on a graph, like a plump maternal line of hills. Now, at last, he was rich in fact as he had always been in fiction. His dreams, blind and misguided as they were, had a chance to come true. Doctor Copper took a holiday in Prague, came to an inner stop, covered his books with cellophane, and then retired to a manor house in his native town. His lotions, powders, and calomel were locked away in a glass-fronted cupboard, and he became the perfect country gentleman, eating long spoons of marmalade for breakfast and thundering about the narrow blossom-infested lanes in a car too old by half, with bright badges on the radiator. He liked his hypocrisy and his gin and his skin which represented culture. Every evening he played croquet and in the mornings he took exercise in Noah's Ark, a rowing-boat contraption which a man in a green suit had installed in the billiards room. He washed his hands regularly in a solution of arsenic and hot water. He was reasonable.

Through many years of medical dictatorship, the doctor had contracted bachelor habits. The traditional picture of the bachelor—a bit crusty, refusing the servitude of slippers, reading Loeb propped against the cruet—fitted in with his imagination of the man comforted by wise finances, the man he had desired to be and now was. He did not mind society (this was how he put it), he did not mind society as an occasional variation. But the essential theme was a dedicated loneliness. Or a dedication to aloneness. He was not quite sure which. Either way, he had his house and many responsibilities.

On summer evenings, the crickets making their noise, the sprinkler busy on the lawn, the doctor liked to stand with silver bands biting into his puffy white sleeves and snip at the privet hedge with flashing shears. Flowers grew at curious angles in his garden. The elms leaned. The waterlilies had distorted leering mouths. This was because he could not bear things to be straight. His pride was a sunflower which he had trained to go round and round like a corkscrew, by dint of patient experiment in a damp dark room with tricks of light and water. By this mild kind of outrage, the doctor kept alive his small scientific vocation. He held that the scientist was by definition religious, attuned to discovery and control, a partner with God in the redemption of chaos. He had quiet delight in his civilised conscience, however, and knew about Auschwitz. He regarded the money part of his mind as a decent corrective, a discipline. Without it, he thought, he could so easily have ended up sacrificing himself to himself in a clinic in Africa, or finding cosmic significance in the number of volts necessary to resuscitate the liver of a dead frog, or scraping the dirt from criminal brains. His interest in the world of bonds and dividends precluded ruthlessness. It was an important link with fallen creation. It made him one with the flaw of the world, and he was glad of this even though he knew that all through his life he had been shocking his fellow healers, and puzzling the sick, by the copy of the *Financial Times* which he sported in the righthand pocket of his shaggy jacket.

In his person, Doctor Copper was tall and fat, with a face like a ripe avocado pear turned upside down, and watchful grey eyes that watered frequently. His carriage, slightly bent, his blue coat buttoned high, with a black silk cravat and austere sidewhiskers, slightly curling, spoke of accomplishments that strictly speaking were not his by right. He had a big slack mouth and bad teeth, babyish hands and an attitude of unalterable melancholy. Although they were rotting, Doctor Copper cleaned his teeth three times a day with cotton wool and peroxide, and gave his gums a whisky massage. He smoked cheroots and enjoyed spitting a little blood.

Thus settled in the country, he decided that some measured liberality was perhaps in order—he had no wish to be remembered as a miser. Elaborate parties for the poor were not in his style of heart, and he could not abide children long enough to affect the successful bestowal of sweets in the street, so he took to patronising by sudden cheques the various causes offering opportunity for salvation in the town. Doctor Copper was not interested in salvation but in this way he did become the saviour of the local church, whose hideous mock-Gothic tower was repaired thanks to his generosity, and the asylum found itself able to open a new wing for the incurably disturbed. He did not keep open house; indeed, he was not known to encourage visitors at all, and his bitch mastiff, Rhawn, never made welcome anyone who ventured unannounced within the gates of Rock House. All the same, in a year or two he was respectfully thought of in the parish of Garthbeibio. He had been mentioned twice in sermons by the Rev Cadog Powys, whose services he attended three times a year, regularly, on Good Friday, All Saints Day, and at midnight on the eve of Christmas, in the church that shone white through the elm trees at the top of the hill. His name and the extent of his charity were recorded in spidery gilt letters on the wall of the asylum waitingroom. And he had opened the county flower show—an act of considerable courage, since the sight of so many unashamedly erect flowers offended him, and he had needed dark glasses in order to complete the ceremony and award prizes to the rose growers.

Every day he took his exercise in Noah's Ark and studied

the tremblings of his shares and bathed in essence of pine and smoked seven cheroots. In this way, several years passed.

Then, one evening in the autumn of perhaps the sixth year of his residence in the parish, the doctor noticed a doll's house in the window of the town's only antique shop. It was a charmingly constructed thing. There were three floors, tiny bulging windows like the eyes of certain circus ponies, and a gabled roof. The furniture was ornate and particular. Candles could be lit within the windows, and a favourite doll set between the candleflame and the glass so that a delicate flickering silhouette appeared thoughtfully and even seemed to make a definite gesture of welcome or dismay if you approached the house from an oblique angle. A set of dolls, three girls with sister faces, dressed in high Victorian costume, went with the house.

Standing in the dusky street, a leaf stuck to the blunt toe-cap of his left boot where it chafed its fellow, Doctor Copper was filled with an unscrupulous excitement as he gazed at the dolls and the doll's house. His hands trembled with the lapels of his blue coat. His knuckles showed white as chicken bones through the creaseless pink of his flesh as he gripped tight his slightly crooked walkingstick and tapped with the horn knob of it against his rotting teeth. His breath came quick and sour. He was seeking, by a complicated mathematical stratagem, to control his mounting passion. An ecstasy of malignant vindictiveness towards all fragility flowed through him. He wanted to smash the thick green glass of the antique shop window, seize the house, and pillage it.

However, his concentration on the difficult piece of mathematics worked as he had hoped it would, and he eventually mastered himself sufficiently to go into the shop and purchase the doll's house and the dolls at what he judged to be a reasonable price, considering his need.

He installed the new toy in his bedroom and for a while all went swimmingly. But when the winter and spring had gone by, and summer came again, with its sullen heat pressing

110

down on the high crumbling sills of the manor house, and the bitter crying of plovers, and the doorknobs all sweaty to the touch, Doctor Copper grew dissatisfied. It was not the doll's house which had lost its charm. No, that still intrigued his senses quite comfortably, on the whole, though he was sometimes to be irritated by the peeling pink paint coming off under his fingers like a scab when he manipulated the tiny silver catches on the windows in setting all the candles in place so that the thing blazed, like a mass or a weddingcake, in the gold and latticed gloom of his sleeping chamber. Not the doll's house, but the dolls, had begun to pall. He had to confess that he no longer felt the thrill, the exquisite shiver, the quickening pulse and melting knees he first had felt in handling the little redcheeked beauties. Yet the dolls themselves had not changed. They were dainty, delicate, adorable as ever. Their cheeks and thighs were cool and smooth and polished to the touch. Their silhouettes were as promising as they had always been. Doctor Copper could not understand the nature of his disenchantment. He soaped his cheeks with Palmolive and left drawers open. With a sigh not altogether sad, he concluded that he must be growing old.

This conclusion was a signal to him to begin indulging his body in ways he had avoided before. From that day forth he was no longer content with cheroots only, but found a sly selfabusive use for his cigarcases. Noah's Ark knew him no more, its oars were neglected, the rowlocks soon rusted. He still found time to trim his shrubs and bushes, and keep his flowers crooked, but the level of gin fell so rapidly in the bottle each day that his childish hands were no longer to be trusted, and meaningless wounds began to appear in the hedge.

It was the time of the hay harvest. Through the lanes about Rock House, which stood as at the centre of a maze, had gone tall lumbering loads, great gentle horses towing the summer home, leaving, amidst wild roses and the honeysuckle,

111

fragrant prickly wisps of hay. Sitting somewhat drunk at his window, exhausted by the smell of crops, sipping a cigar and spitting now and again in a little silver cup, the doctor was gloomily admiring the sun and assessing its corrupt influence on his begonias, when he saw a man drive a motorcycle through one of the holes in the hedge and zoom towards him across the lawn.

The mastiff bitch, Rhawn, leaped dutifully at the intruder's throat. The front wheel struck her and she was killed on the instant. The huge black machine turned over, its rider got up no worse for the spill, kicked at the dog, ignored it, and started dusting down his leathers, which were rusty black and worn with much travel.

Doctor Copper's first thought was to telephone for the police. But, on reflection, he beckoned the newcomer to him and poured him a large gin.

The man gulped it down thirstily. Doctor Copper observed that he had a narrow waist and a black patch over one eye. When the gin was gone his good eye shone.

Dear sir, he began, much as I hate the risk of boring you I must describe my heart to a certain extent in order to show you what a difference your hospitality has made and to answer your questions.

Thinly depressed by this outburst, the doctor contented himself with pointing out that he had not yet asked any questions.

The stranger shrugged. He had, Doctor Copper noticed, a cosmopolitan way with his shoulders. I will try to please you as little as possible, he promised. He accepted a cheroot and went on talking with it in his mouth as the doctor struck matches to get it going for him.

Comrade, said the stranger, perspective I am sure you will agree is important in any complex. I will not merely begin at the beginning, therefore, I will begin before the beginning. Open the eyes of your ears, my friend, and I will tell you a lie about a much more lovable person than Gerard Benjamin,

112

who hails in any case from a country that has not yet been discovered.

The cigar was alight. The doctor pocketed the cigarcase. That is your name? he said politely. Gerard Benjamin?

The motorcyclist smiled. The smile expressed no opinion. He leaned forwards. His eyepatch winked cruelly in the sun. Chatterton was not mad, he whispered.

I never supposed he was, said the doctor.

My father's father, the motorcyclist went on, was the Old Testament in trousers. His beard was like yours, only white.

Doctor Copper put his hand to his chin and was startled to find that he *had* a beard. It had not been there the last time he looked in the mirror—but he could not remember how long ago that was.

If the man who appeared to have referred to himself as Gerard Benjamin observed the doctor's surprise, he did not show it. Despite some sad experiences with sixpenny whores, he said ruminatively, puffing round his cigar, Grumph still had a monopolist's faith in Progress. I suppose you could put it down to the nineteenth century, ah me, that long, long nineteenth century, longer than the eighteenth and the seventeenth laid end to end. As for the sixteenth . . .

He laughed. The effect was waspish.

It hardly counts at all, offered the doctor, and then fell silent, dismayed by his anxiety to flatter.

If you like, said the motorcyclist ungratefully. Well, what do they say, old boy? What do they all say? If Chatterton was not mad, he must have been starving, that's what. Biographers weep. It's what they want. A handkerchief maker cashes in with a hanky depicting The Distressed Poet (alternative colours, red or blue) in sorry apartment with folded bed, the broken utensil below it, bottle, farthing candle, the disorderly raiment of the bard. I ask you, old boy, I ask you, is this a true picture?

Doctor Copper said it very probably was not. His opinion

113

on the subject was unchanged by the handkerchief (blue) which Mr Benjamin offered him in illustration.

Rocks, said Mr Benjamin, rocks, clocks, shells, stuffed tigers, pedometers, double needle telegraphs in mahogany cases, stereoscopic cameras, a Holtzappfel lathe, every kind of scope and gram you could think of or have never even heard of—

What on earth are you talking about? the doctor demanded.

My paternal grandfather's house, said Mr Benjamin. The place was a sort of poor man's version of the Goethe museum at Weimar.

Goethe? the doctor said indignantly.

You heard me, said Mr Benjamin. Bloody bleeding Goethe. He clenched his cigar between his teeth as he fumbled with a zip on the leg of his leathers. It opened and he plunged his hand into a deep pocket. When he took his hand out again he was holding a microscope.

A family heirloom, he explained.

He gave the instrument gently to the doctor.

Doctor Copper peered at it. Engraved on its body were the words IMPROVED COMPOUND MICROSCOPE, *made only by M. L. Probus, Old Compton St., Soho.* I like that made only by, he commented, for something to say. He was wondering how the thing had escaped injury in the crash.

Mr Benjamin tapped his eyepatch. It made a singing sound. Grumph used that instrument, he went on, in his Chatterton researches.

Fancy, said the doctor.

When he was a young man, Mr Benjamin explained, he worked as a porter in the Saracen's Head Tap, Skinner Street. One morning he woke up with these words on his lips: How could Chatterton *afford* to buy arsenic from Cross the apothecary?

A question I've often asked myself, sneered the doctor, especially when there is no R in the month. Now, if you will forgive me . . .

Anything, said Mr Benjamin. That's what I'm for.

114

Doctor Copper bit his lip. It tasted of onions. He fell silent.

My grandfather deduced, Mr Benjamin went on, that the true reasons for Chatterton's suicide had been hushed up. He left his post at the Saracen's Head Tap and went to live next door to a Mr Stephens, inventor of a now wellknown ink. His neighbour on the other side was a gentleman also connected with ink, being destined to put several gallons of it to good use.

He drew on his cigar without apparent hunger. In case you're wondering about the gallons of ink gentleman, he said, it was a certain henpecked Mr Dickens.

Doctor Copper dropped the microscope as though it had been revealed to him that the thing was smeared with the germ of a rare disease. It smashed on the terrace floor. He expected the stranger to show anger, and began to apologise, but then stopped as the other merely nodded, staring at the sun with his one unencumbered eye.

Death's chamberlains, he said, that's what the Bristol people called the Chattertons. Oh, my father's father soon had all the bloody facts at his disposal. He found out about Chatterton Senior, for instance, how he had a mouth so wide you could put your clenched fist in it, and sang in the cathedral, and studied Cornelius Agrippa. And how young Tom went to Colston's, where three years before a pupil had been expelled for a leprosy. And about that swine, the man-midwife Barrett. And Mrs Balance, and poets hating brooms, and all the rest of it. He got the facts in order, did Grumph. Then he turned to the known clues—the Rowley poems.

Chatterton's forgeries? queried Doctor Copper, who knew a little.

Mr Benjamin flicked ash from his cigar. Shit, he said.

I beg your pardon? snapped Doctor Copper.

Of course, said Mr Benjamin. He leaned forwards eagerly. Never bolt your door with a boiled carrot, he advised. He nodded as if keeping time with the rhythm of his own thoughts.

115

No one eats goldfish nowadays, he went on. You notice that, comrade? Ah well, every bloody path has its bloody puddle, and every bloody poet feels a fraud, I daresay, to the extent that his inspiration is honest. The more honest the inspiration, the more dishonest the poet feels, taking credit for what he writes, eh? Liars have short wings, at all events, and to relieve this tedium—of embarrassing your own poems—by pretending they are by someone else is just to declare in fiction what you feel them to be in fact. Chatterton *was* Rowley, so far as he had any identity at all. A fool could see that. You've only got to compare a Rowley poem with a non-Rowley poem.

Good God, cried the doctor, I do hope not!

Hope? Hope's as cheap as despair, said Mr Benjamin. He rubbed his right forefinger round the inside of his glass, collecting a last lick of gin, which he took with a grimace. Christ, he said, I'll be glad when we've had enough of this.

Doctor Copper was beginning to be bored by his visitor's distressing sincerity. He wished the fellow would go away so that he could retire to the bathroom with the fresh cigarcase which he had been surreptitiously stroking in his pocket. To his horror, however, he found himself pouring the man another drink.

Mr Benjamin settled back comfortably, cradling the glass. How bloody good it is to give the Holy Sacrament! he remarked. The lips seem dead without it, the heart blind. The voice, it has no words to say. The ears, no songs to hear. The sacrament makes us and wakes us, who give, who take.

He formed his thumb and finger into a circle, blew cigar smoke through it, and winked his good eye at the doctor. Bottoms up! he piped. The wise man's passion!

Doctor Copper coughed. Am I to understand, he began.

No need, said Mr. Benjamin. Believe in witchcraft?

The doctor said he did not but he might.

116

Mr Benjamin shook his head at caution. All lies, he said. Lies, dear sir, and humbug.

You are an atheist? asked Doctor Copper.

His guest made an evasive noise through his nostrils. Ever read Johannem Wierum? he demanded.

The doctor admitted that he had not.

Proves it, said Mr Benjamin, smoothing his rusty leathers with a gin-filmed finger, proves it beyond a shadow of a doubt. Of course, I'd be the first to admit that truth doesn't always seem true. But look, you don't have to read at all, tell you what happened to me once, at Wittenburg. Captain in the Imperial Guard, so much make-up on his face you'd think his eyes were on upside-down, just mounted his steed at the Elster Gate, to inspect the bloody flag, when his horse starts to rear and rage, shake its silly head, snort, roar, run—not, if you see what I mean, as horses are supposed to do, neighing and all that, but in a voice like a woman's. Mezzo soprano, as a matter of fact. Well, yours truly was the only one there who didn't think the devil had a hoof in it. General confusion. As for the horse, it throws the captain off, trots on his skull, kicks, rolls, jumps, would have killed him if I hadn't put a bullet up its arse.

Cruel, murmured Doctor Copper.

Not at all, said Mr Benjamin, not a bit of it. I'd seen the pink smoke coming from its nostrils, hadn't I? Had to act quick. Bent down and saw I was right. A lunt up the bugger's nose.

A lunt? said Doctor Copper.

Almost as long as your left forefinger, yes, said his visitor. Still burning. Some joker poked it up there with a needle. Nasty, very. Turned out to be the captain's groom, as a matter of fact. Christ, should have heard the poor devil scream when they caught him! Captain had his balls for breakfast. Poached. On toast.

Man is what he eats, said Doctor Copper, blushing. He quickly changed the subject. I see, he said, that you have a rather nasty lump behind your ear. Perhaps you injured your-self when your machine stopped? I had better examine you.

You had better not, said Mr Benjamin. I got that bump yesterday. Little accident. Went into the station and paid my penny for a wash-up. The seat fell on my head.

Doctor Copper swallowed hard. A shadow passed across the sun. The mouths in the hedge gaped wide. The doctor shivered.

Mr Benjamin was finishing his drink with a gesture like a hypnotist's. But I digress, he chuckled. Where was I?

About your father's father, suggested Doctor Copper, and plumed himself on his politeness.

Naturally, said Mr Benjamin. Raw dads make fat lads, what? Consider, Grumph now had three clues re the Chatterton case. One, Chatterton was marvellous, two, he was a boy, three, his cousin said he never slept much. He got to work on these with his intuition and soon came up with some interesting data. One, Chatterton held that the greatest oath a man could swear was by the honour of his ancestors—

Such as? queried the doctor surlily.

Such as . . . Such as . . . Such as, By my grandmother's tobacco pipe! said Mr Benjamin.

A smart piece of humanism, admitted the doctor.

Two, said Mr Benjamin, he had written anecdotes from the low Dutch and signed them ECNUD SUTOCS. Three, he once sent a letter which began, Damn the Muses.

It's all experience, offered Doctor Copper, and was again alarmed by his sycophancy.

There was a short silence. A wasp had settled on the bruise of a fallen peach. Doctor Copper watched it without amuse-ment. He realised that he had never in his life been anything but an amateur. The wasp, however, was a professional. He hated it. He pitied it, also, for its lack of subtlety.

Mr Benjamin was speaking. One should refrain, he said, from criticising a dictionary for not being an encyclopaedia.

Doctor Copper did not know how to argue with this,

although in his present mood he felt like it. He was beginning to long for his dolls. The fury of the longing took him by surprise, he had thought all that was over for ever. He was not altogether pleased to find the old need returning, but imagination instructing him so hotly in new things he could do, he found it hard to concentrate on what his guest was saying, which in any case was only that Chatterton's passion for words had led him virtually to invent a new language for his own purposes out of such linguistic scraps as came to hand, principally a couple of dictionaries he scarcely understood and a copy of Chaucer in which his favourite poem seems to have been the glossary.

It might kill them, said Doctor Copper.

His visitor folded his hands. The doctor recognised the gesture. It was just that kind of selfscrubbing a priest does under the white of his long sleeves.

Did I ever tell you, asked Mr Benjamin, about the time I rogered me jolly way out of the snowdrift? I'd seen the wall of snow sliding down towards the road, but it was so quiet, sir, so damnably white and quiet, that I didn't realise the danger. The valley seemed all right. About halfway through I heard this rumbling to my left. Up on the hillside, I saw the wall moving down towards the road again. Before I had time to react the snow was heading straight towards me. It galloped. It fell. In three seconds it swept across me, knocking me over, humming, drumming, rucksacks, suitcases, the lot. Snow covered me. Complete snow, completely, covered. I couldn't believe it had happened until I heard Madame Saba and Duncan Kilduff shouting for help. Help, help. They shouted. Help. After a couple of minutes, after a minute or two, the shouting stopped. It stopped. Of course I'd read books on what to do when caught in an avalanche. The victim should thrash his arms and legs about and try to swim through it. But this snow was already still. Static snow, a gather of fact, a snow of statistics, drifted, and yours faithfully had lost his bloody drift in it. I was trapped, helpless, trapped, helpless,

119

trapped, gasping for air, breathing at four times the normal rate, a bladder of lard, bladder of lard, terrible. Well, sport, I thought to myself, if you can make a space above your head it will create a pocket or envelope of air, enough to allow you to breathe, letting enough air to breathe in. A paradigm of our condition, yes siree. Well, for the next half hour, old boy, I was facing facts, I can tell you. For the next half hour I was moving my arm back and forth, back and forth above my head, above my curly head, pushing the snow back inch by inch by inch. Eventually there was this little dome of space above me. My breathing, you will be glad to hear, became easier. Life bloomed. The snow was rosy. I started to enjoy myself. I started working snow down from round the area of my head and shoulders, working it down towards my feet, trampling it, down, down, down. My clothes by this time were soaking and my arms and legs were pretty stiff. My shirt hurt. Frostbite gnawed at my hands and feet. Still, more and more air was filtering into the little cavern I was making. Believe me, I congratulated myself on paying seventeen pounds for a pair of good ski-boots. Those boots were in fact priceless. Without them I would be sitting here now without toes or even without feet. A toeless Benjamin, Gerard footless, unimaginable, what? Your author would have given up had his creature not purchased a pair of stout sturdy ski-boots for seventeen pounds eleven shillings and fivepence in Princes Street. A bargain at the price. You'll be asking yourself what else I was wearing. I'll tell you. A woollen polo-neck sweater, a good anorak, and blue ski trousers. Now you're in the picture. Next thing I did was to start exercising my fingers to prevent them stiffening up altogether. I clenched my fist rapidly fifty times with one hand, then the same with the other. I did this hour after hour in between scraping away more and more snow. Then I heard this noise in the distance. It came louder. Naturally, old sport, I rather wondered what it was. Then I knew what it was. A shiver travelled through the snow, a roar, a grumble, a shout, a rumble, a spreading fury or flurry

120

or perturbation of cracks spiderwebbing. It was a snowplough. My heart stood still. I took it out and adjusted it. Then I stitched it to the arm of my good anorak, between the other badges. So, so, a snowplough. I imagined its great tall mincer blades slicing and whipping up the snow and throwing it to the roadside. Crunch-scrunch of a walk through snow, the crisp imprint of boot, heel-dig, toecap-scribble, the after-slide of the smooth sole where the sun has smoothed the surface an inch down. Following across the fields, one foot after another, in his master's steps, my own steps up for the milk and back again, across the sloping field in the Decembering sun, the milkbottles with long tongues of cream sticking from the tops of them. How I would kneel and suck that ice! But, now, to business. The snowplough. The mincing machine crashfucking through snowballs, thud of blade and whirl of flake. It could cut me in half, and I was by no means sure which half I liked the better. Still, not to worry, it didn't. Panic over. Six or seven hours passed. Night came through the snow. I settled down comfortably to my exercises. I managed to pull my lighter from my rucksack, which was still on my back. I realised of course that the flame would burn up vital oxygen, but I thought it worth the risk if a little warmth was to be got from it. Alas, my hands were bum numb and I couldn't get the bloody thing to work. My next move was to try to get the rucksack from my back and the baton from it. I would conduct the snow. Major manœuvres in the snow. A symphony of snowwhirl. Mass in B. Missa solemnis. No. Alack. It couldn't be done. I fumbled inside for my gloves and food. I inched my elbows through the straps. I found it made things easier if I rolled up my sleeves to do this. It took me two hours. The time passed. Night had come, falling through the snow, dark through the snow, night. I was tired. I dropped off to sleep and dreamt of Madame Saba. When I woke up I had a hard on. I thrust cautiously. My pecker swelled and melted snow to right and left. At last I knew the answer! The heat of my pole would make me a hole! Comrade, I con-

centrated hard, believe me. I worked. I pumped. I pressed. I
gave my all. More snow melted. My wee propeller was smoking, sir, smoking. I fanned it as a cowboy fans his Colt. Satisfied
snow fell away from it, glistening globules of snow, melting,
going. I tried some more. Fantasy, you understand, was
required. Pangfuck farted on the sacred relics. Bugger me,
begged Madame Saba. The butler stripped his prick and lit it
with a Swan Vesta. It burned with a dim religious light, glue-
blue in gloom, accumulated. These are my collected sperms, he
announced, glorying in the echoes, my name is Tool. The snow
was going! It was definitely going! My swelling cockerel of a
cock was carolling through cold, welding or wielding a shaft of
heat through the packed white drift. Encouraged, in the name
of survival and evolution, I increased the pressure, turned on
the heat. It was hard work, my friend. I stuck to it. I did not
flinch. I did my duty. Madame Sodom, the butler announced,
and Lord Tool. The snow was certainly moving now. I could
feel it all about me, changed to warmth. I was making love
to the frozen air, to the earth, to the wind and the rain and
the stopped sun and the moon, a melting moon that was all
about me. I was making love to a moment of time. Sperm and
snow! Sperm and snow! I was all aglow, sir. At last I had
a purpose in life : to fuck my way out of it. Ah, the long
years of longing were worth it now. At last I'd found a need
adequate to my expression. If only I could keep my furniture erect it would act like a blowlamp and blow me from
the drift! It was a torch, a shaft, a bonfire, a beacon, a weapon
of fire, a burning spear, a flaming arrow from the bow of
my sweating hairy loins, and by its power I might propel
myself free, edge and inch my way out, escape from the tomb
on the rocket of the race! At last a use for imagination. It
was in the service of survival. Without fantasies I could not
prevail. That they were not my fantasies did not matter. All
the fantasies were one sickness. The sickness was the way it
was. And there was snow to melt. Echoes bowed before me.
I scrubbed, sir. It was raw now. But I had to go on, I had
122

to go on. Deeper yet, my hard heart, ruthlessly. He stuck, the young Lord Tool, a fat Havana cigar, with a gold band, into the cunt of the maid who lay beside him. Laughing, she lit and smoked it. I indulged myself, sir, in hatred of this snow, these echoes of innocence. My energy was iconoclastic, almost. The drift was one fat sugary kiss. I addressed myself utterly to the task of destroying the last relics of its virginity. I worked like a Turk, sir. No woman was ever screwed half as hard as your humble servant screwed that snowdrift. On and on and on and on and on and on and in and on and on and in and in and in and in and in and in and out then out and out and out and out and out. Out. Out. Out. Well, sir, well, the hole I had made was now about six inches in diameter and nearly six feet long. I took up my gloves again and put one of them on my right hand and the other on my engine, and I ate an apple and an orange. Then I wrapped a towel round my throat, picked up a shoe from the rucksack and started to scrape away at the hole I had punctured in the snow. The gloves brought me a lot of relief, even though one of them would not go on properly, my hand was too swollen, my right hand, as I say. But I felt confident now. That was the important thing. I kept on scraping the snow and tramping it down with my feet. Slowly I worked my way to the surface. Twenty-four hours after the avalanche had engulfed him, yours sincerely broke through! I pushed my head and shoulders out of the snow and gulped in great good lungfuls of wonderful air! I looked about me. I took stock of my situation. I was half-way up the drift. Now, I thought, I must try to put the past behind me. I waved at a passing lorry. The lorry driver waved back, but did not stop.

Doctor Copper looked at his oblique begonias for relief, but there was none. He had been thinking, during the greater part of this outburst, of his shares. He had more or less made up his mind to sell the dollar stock, the laundrette, and the Aus-

123

tralian mines. This helped. His guest did not seem to have noticed his inattention. Anyone for poetry? he demanded.

Doctor Copper grinned. He felt as though his grave had been opened, and for no good reason.

You're not a member of the mafia then? said Mr Benjamin.

Mafia? said Doctor Copper.

The P.R.B., hissed Mr Benjamin. He crossed himself at top speed, but seemed disappointed when the doctor stared at him without understanding. There was a moment's silence, then, tapping his patch, Mr Benjamin went on: Grumph and Mr Dickens had to consider the case of Peter Smith. The sea refuses no river. Smith was a boy who killed himself in Bristol in the summer of 1769, one of three Smith brothers who were friends of Chatterton's. There's an account of them in the *Gentleman's Magazine*, December issue, 1838. Citizen, I quote: Peter Smith was another *bon compagnon*, and incurred by his irregularities with Chatterton, the displeasure of his father, so that he was most severely lectured, of which such was the effect, that he retired to his chamber, and set his associate an example that was but too soon followed. Richard Smith—blah, blah, shit, shit, oh yes, I thought it would be over here—Richard Smith and Chatterton were good friends, but the unhappy affair of his brother Peter estranged them, as Richard attributed the wretched catastrophe to congenial opinions in morals and religion. William Bradford Smith was Chatterton's bosom friend.

He had been reciting from memory, although his whole manner was that of a man who consults a text. Now he stopped and stared at the doctor with a flickering smile. There is no reason to doubt this, he said.

Damn it, said Doctor Copper, I don't.

Consider, invited Mr Benjamin, two letters written to Chatterton by women. The first was in the British Museum until this morning.

He took a piece of crumpled paper from the big pocket on his thigh and handed it to the doctor, who read as follows:

124

Sir
I send my Love to you and Tell you Thiss
if you prove Constant I not miss
but if you frown and torn a way
I can make Cart of better Hay
pray Excep of me Love Hartley
an send me word Cartingley
Tell me how maney ounces of Gre'
n Ginger Bread can show the Baker of Honiste
My house is not bilt with Stavis
I not be Coarted by Boys nor Navis
I Haive a man an man shall Haive me
if I whaint a fool I send for thee
if you are going to the D
I wish you a good Gonery.

What do you think of that? demanded Mr Benjamin.

It has nice legs, said Doctor Copper.

Thank you, said Mr Benjamin, but it's what the poet himself has scribbled on the back that is really interesting. Look and see!

The doctor looked. He saw:

> Go suck green sickness girls and wenches
> On Bulks in Lanes on Tombs and Benches.

He said, We should destroy this.

As you please, said Mr Benjamin, but you and I, dear sir, are the only people in the universe who know of it.

Perhaps God? suggested Doctor Copper.

No, said Mr Benjamin, I have not told Him.

I see, said Doctor Copper. You are a philosopher.

A good head, said Mr Benjamin, gets itself hats. The second letter, he shouted.

He took it from his pocket, and Doctor Copper read:

Sir
to a Blage you I wright a few Lines to you But have

125

not the weakness to be Believe all you say of me for
you may say as much to other young Ladys for all I
now But I Can't go out of a Sunday with you for I
ham a fraid we Shall be seen toge Sir if it agreeable
to you I had Take a walk with you in the morning
for I be Belive we shant be seen a bout 6 a Clock But
we must wait with patient for there is a Time for all
Things

ESTHER SAUNDERS

Mr Benjamin snatched the letter back and waved it over
his head. Again, he cried, an annotation by T.C.! This time
he has written: There is a time for all things—except marriage, my dear.

Doctor Copper nodded. He was not disposed to commit
another imprudence. He was not going to fret about Chatterton any more than he was going to fret about snowdrifts. He
was thinking that he could make a new set of underwear for
each of his dolls, and that if he made this flimsy and modern
it would provide a piquant contrast with their outer, Victorian
things when he lifted up their dresses. He sucked his bad teeth
at the prospect.

Mr Benjamin began to pace up and down the terrace
rudely, swinging his hands from the wrists. Do you realise, he
said, that if you go for girls with big bums, bin bums, jolly
bums, it means you've a passion for patience?

What about small bums, bun bums, misery bums? said the
doctor weakly.

Shows you're not guilt-ridden, said his guest. He spat out the
consonants like broken glass. Then, Gentleman of the jury,
he declaimed, let us forget all the nonsense that has been
written about Chatterton's last days by people being wise after
the event, and consider, as Grumph and Mr Dickens considered, the last letter the boy wrote. This is nobody's opinion

126

but his own, and therefore the only thing of value in assessing the reasons for his suicide.

Don't you think it might have been murder? Doctor Copper demanded slyly.

No, said Mr Benjamin, I don't.

And your paternal grandfather? said Doctor Copper.

He didn't either, said Mr Benjamin.

And Mr. Dickens? said Doctor Copper.

That twerp, said Mr Benjamin.

Doctor Copper sighed. Another drink? he offered. He wanted to be rid of the fellow. His fingers itched to be at the dolls.

Alas, his guest took him seriously, and held out his glass to be filled. To Thomas Chatterton, he declared, by a long and forgotten parentage, the posthumous father of Sprung Rhythm.

You have killed my dog, said Doctor Copper.

It was the first major criticism he had allowed himself. Mr. Benjamin ignored it. He beamed like a malevolent teapot. On the way here this evening, he said, I knocked down two book-makers. So I took them into a field, dug a hole, and buried them.

Dug a hole and buried them? said Doctor Copper. My God, man, are you sure they were dead?

One of them said he wasn't, said Mr Benjamin, but you know what liars bookmakers are.

He shrugged. The letter is here, he said. Tattooed across my buttocks.

He slipped off his leathers. He was naked underneath, and the doctor read as follows:

> Infallible Doctor,
> Let this apologise for long silence. Your request would have been long since granted but I know not what it is best to compose: a Hendecasyllabum carmen, Hexastichon, Ogdastich, Tetrametrum or Septenarius. You must

127

know that I have long been troubled with a poetical
Cephalophonia, for I no sooner begin an Acrostick, but
I wander into a Threnodia. The poem ran thus: the
first line, an Acatalectos; the second an Aetiologia of the
first; the third an Acyrologia; the fourth an Epanalepsis
of the third; the fifth, a Diatyposis of beauty; sixth, a
Diaporesis of success; seventh, a Brachycatalecton; eighth,
an Ecphonesis of Ecplexis. In short, an Emporium could
not contain a greater Synchysis of such accidents without
Syzygia. I am resolved to forsake the Parnassian Mount,
and would advise you to do so too, *and attain the mystery
of composing Smegma.* Think not I make a Mycterismus
in mentioning *Smegma.* No; my Mnemosyne will let me
see (unless I have an Amblyopia) your great services,
which will always be remembered by

HASMOT ETCHAORNTT

The italics are mine, Mr Benjamin explained modestly, pull-
ing up his trousers.

Doctor Copper sank back and mopped his brow. He found
himself without a word to say.

That last letter, Mr Benjamin continued, is undated as you
will have noticed, but I can assure you that it was written a
fortnight before the end. It was addressed to William Smith,
the one Chatterton loved beyond the love which tenderest
brothers bear. Do you find it unintelligible?

I shall see my solicitors, said Doctor Copper weakly.

Grumph did, said Mr. Benjamin, until he had Mr Dickens
examine it under the optical microscope. Then they made
their great discovery. Truth never grows old! The Chatterton case was solved!

His voice was getting into top gear again. His mouth was
an unsewn wound. Doctor Copper clenched his walkingstick
in his babyish hands and glared hopelessly at the sun.

Mr Benjamin said: Before I tell you what their discovery
was, sir—some advice. Follow the sheilas? Of course you do!

128

Well, let me take the hard work out of it for you. I know of one certain winner for next Saturday. A calculated cool coup. A horse the colour of treacle toffee. Connections are planning to have it off, my boy. An armchair ride, game, genuine, and consistent. One of the most honest animals ever to leer through a bridle. Manufactures his own cortisol too. In perfect trim, and out to win. He'll fairly canter at his rivals, you see. My information is absolutely inspired and I know all there is to know about the game. You don't want to lose races by the length of a cheap cigar? You want considered certainties all set to score? One hundred per cent triers, trained to the minute and cleverly placed by one of the shrewdest stables in the business, people who make no mistakes when the chips are down? Well, I'm your man. Please note that I don't indulge in the practice of following up losers when next they run, for how on earth can anyone know what they will be up against in opposition—anyway, who wants too many losers?

You are a tipster? said Doctor Copper.

I am aware, said Mr Benjamin, that you are interested in making racing pay and that you are interested in a genuine advisory service that gives clients exactly what they pay for. Well, you must come to me in the end! Do you know why?

I do not, said Doctor Copper.

I'll tell you, said Mr Benjamin. You are a master of your trade as I am of mine. Let's put it this way. Say, for example, I want a house built, the first thing required after the purchase of the land is a suitable plan of the house. Do I attempt to plan this house myself? Not on your sweet life, I don't, it's not my line of business and for another thing I can't bloody draw, can I? So what do I do? I go to a qualified architect and for a fee he designs a house that I really want. Next comes the building of the house, do I build it? The answer is no, I haven't the faintest clue about building, so I go to a reputable builder who knows his job and he builds it. The point is this— with my vast knowledge and resources at your disposal for an agreed fee you come to me for advice. I am master of my trade as you are of yours. I do hope you see my point. I think that puts things in a nutshell.

To bet or not to bet, said Doctor Copper, that is the question. Whether 'tis nobler in the mind to suffer the slings and arrows of outrageous fortune in the shape of slow horses on fast courses, or by bookmaking end them. Neither, thanks, I'll stick to stocks.

Embarrassed lest this short flight of eloquence had betrayed rather more than the fact of his unalterable boredom, the doctor started playing churches with his fingers. He opened his hands. But there was no choir.

Mr Benjamin shrugged. On the night of the 24th of August, 1770, he said, Chatterton goes to his expensive garret early and locks the door. When repeated knockings bring no reply next day, that door is broken down. The floor is covered with a carpet of pieces of paper, no bigger than sixpences. Chatterton's body is a most horrid spectacle, with limbs and features distorted as after convulsions, a frightful and ghastly corpse. The inquest—

No, said Doctor Copper, no, no.

The inquest, said Mr Benjamin.

For the love of heaven, said Doctor Copper, spare me the inquest.

For the love of heaven, said Mr Benjamin, I may not spare you anything. The inquest, as I was saying, brings in a verdict that he has swallowed arsenic in water on the 24th August, 1770, and died, in consequence thereof, the next day. The body is then thrown in the pit of Shoe Lane Workhouse. His name is entered in the burialbook as William Chatterton.

Poetry, said Doctor Copper, is not what it used to be.

Why did Chatterton kill himself? Mr Benjamin went on grindingly, his eye shining. Grumph and Mr Dickens asked themselves that same question you are asking now. Well, sport, a bald head is soon shaven. They came to the conclusion any honest man must come to. The evidence, dear sir, the bloody evidence all points one way.

He downed his gin in one gulp and smacked his lips. Consider this, he said, while I have another little drink.

The doctor had closed his eyes. When he opened them he found himself looking at a pink mimeographed sheet with deckled edges.

Mr Benjamin poured gin for himself and sipped it absent-mindedly as the doctor read:

DERBY PUZZLE SOLVED!

NOT by PUBLIC FORM, but by PRIVATE home trials!! The SENSATIONAL information I have secured for the DERBY and OAKS is a CLEVERLY KEPT SECRET! These horses will amaze everyone by STREAKING AWAY at the finish!! It's the MOST ASTONISHING news I have EVER HEARD in my thirty odd years as a RACING ADVISER! It's a great pleasure to offer it to every client. I have agreed to pay my TOPHIGHEST FEE for this REMARKABLE news, which ALSO INCLUDES ONE for Epsom's ROYAL HANDICAP on the THURSDAY. All three are EX-CLUSIVE to BENJAMIN and absolutely UNOBTAIN-ABLE ELSEWHERE. I don't want the favourite in these big races. I have THREE SENSATIONAL COUPS TO BEAT THE LOT!! Mark my words. The PREMIER CLASSIC will produce ANOTHER DERBY SUR-PRISE!! A TERRIFIC SENSATION!! I have myself backed these three SMASHERS singly, in mixed doubles and in a grand treble. Yes, and for 10/- ONLY, the GREAT NEWS IS YOURS to do exactly the same and stand to win a PACKET like I do! Whatever you have already backed or intend backing, DON'T BE LEFT OUT OF THIS REMARKABLE OFFER! It's 100% GENUINE!! REMEMBER, THREE HORSES ONLY

131

(I absolutely GUARANTEE this), with all the PRIVATE INSIDE DETAILS! One is in Wednesday's DERBY, ONE in Thursday's ROYAL HANDICAP, and ONE IN FRIDAY'S OAKS—this REALLY is A CHANCE OF A LIFETIME!! Everyone can afford ten bob for TOPCLASS SENSATIONAL NEWS IN DERBY WEEK, so don't hang back as if it's a FORTUNE! Slip away your 10/- NOW—TODAY, and simply include your name and full address. HURRY!—and you can then get on THE EXPECTED DERBY WINNER as the first of THREE REMARKABLE JOBS. (10/- covers EVERYTHING. I pay for all sealed letters and they will arrive in good time). (NOTE.—On similar trebles of mine in the past, clients with one moderate stake have won such sums as

£1818, £1700, £700, £850, £800, etc., etc.) GERARD BENJAMIN has been established and advertising from the same address since 1939.

GERARD BENJAMIN, Horseshoes, Almedore Lane, Newmarket, Suffolk.

The presumed author of this proclamation put his finger to his nose and belched. Then he said : They'll come out of the gate like scalded cats, brother, and never get caught. They've been knocking on the door.

On the door, said Doctor Copper, who has been knocking on the door?

Your horses, said Mr Benjamin.

My horses are knocking on the door, said Doctor Copper.

A phrase of the Turf, Mr Benjamin explained generously. It means the animals in question are ready and waiting to win, and have been going close in their last few races. My Royal Handicap cert, for instance—last time out, Goodwood, six furlongs, he may have resented being steadied after a fast break. He was fairly hacking up below the distance, but then

132

started going backwards a furlong out. He's a lot of room for improvement yet. The going was poached that day. He likes it on top.

On top of what? asked the doctor.

The going, said Mr Benjamin. He likes top of the ground conditions.

Does that imply, said Doctor Copper, that the creature has no deathwish?

He'll come with a wet sail, Mr Benjamin promised. This one could win with his two front legs tied together, you see, sir. Piggott rides.

Doctor Copper delivered himself listlessly of the opinion that ducks lay eggs and geese lay wagers. He looked at the sky. It was now the colour of rain. But no rain fell.

I have long been troubled with a poetical Cephalophonia, recited Mr Benjamin. Now, sirrah, CEPHALALGIA can mean a pain or heaviness in the head. CEPHALOHAEMATOMA is a subcutaneous swelling containing blood. CEPHALOPLEGIA is paralysis of the head and face muscles. What about that? The first line, an Acatalectos . . . Would it surprise you to learn that ACATALECTIC means not catalectic, i.e. a verse with the exact number of syllables the metre requires, without defect or superfluity? But ACATALEPTIC (which is in Bailey's DICTIONARY) means relating to acatalepsy, incomprehensibility. And ACATAPHASIA, master, ACATAPHASIA is the lack of power to express connected thought, associated with some sort of cerebral lesion!

Mr Benjamin was getting more and more excited by what he had to say. Sweat shone on his eyebrows as he continued.

The second an Aetiologia . . . , he screeched. AETIOLOGY is : one, the assignment of a cause; two, the science or philosophy of causation, and three, your honour, three, that branch of medical science which investigates the causes and origin of diseases.

133

He paused for effect.

The doctor took no notice. He was tearing the racing advertisement into tiny pieces. This was difficult, because the paper was thick and sticky.

Mr Benjamin went on: Sixth, a Diaporesis . . . DIAPORESIS is a rhetorical figure, in which the speaker professes to be at a loss, which of two or more causes, statements, etc., to adopt. But DIAPHORESIS is perspiration! And DIAPYESIS is suppuration! Kersey's DICTIONARY has DIAPYETICKS—medicines that cause swellings to suppurate or run with matter, or that ripen and break sores. Imagine Grumph's pleasure when he discovered that Chatterton had a copy of Kersey's! In short, an Emporium . . . Bailey's DICTIONARY (which Chatterton also used, the 1721 edition) gives this meaning which the O.E.D. now notes as obsolete: EMPORIUM—the common sensory of the brain. . . . could not contain a greater Synchysis . . . SYNCHYSIS, as Mr Dickens told Grumph, can mean either, one, a confused arrangement of words in a sentence, that obscures the meaning, or, two, m'lud, two, softening or fluidity of the vitreous humour of the eye, called sparkling synchysis when minute flakes of cholesterin float in the humour, causing a sparkling appearance in the field of vision. Blanchard's PHYSICAL DICTIONARY (1684) gives a preternatural confusion of the blood and humours of the eye. Interesting? Wait for this! Grumph and Mr Dickens called in Mr Stephens. They were now hot on the trail! . . . of such incidents without Syzygia . . . SYZYGY comes from the Greek for copulation! There is also, they discovered, an obsolete meaning of the plural of SYZYGY meaning the pairs of cranial nerves. A 1681 medical dictionary gave them: SYZYGIES—the nerves that carry the sense from the brain to the whole body. And SYZYGY, what's more, usually refers to the fusion of two organisms without loss of identity. A zygote, your grace, formed by the coalition of two similar gametes. (A zygote is the cell resulting from the union of two gametes in sexual bloody reproduction!) SYZYGIA, says Kersey (DICTIONARIUM

134

ANGLOBRITANNICUM, 1708 edition), is a term among grammarians for the coupling or clapping of different feet together in Greek or Latin verse, i.e. dipody, or the combination of two feet in one metre. You see where all this is driving? Where it drove Grumph? And Mr Dickens? And, almost against his will, Mr Stephens too? No. My Mnemosyne (memory) will let me see (unless I have an Amblyopia) . . . AMBLYOPIA is impaired vision, generally from a defective sensibility of the retina, or cloudiness of the media, the early stage of amaurosis. The cause is often ascribed to a lesion of the eye! Phillips (1706) gives AMBLYOPIA—dullness or dimness of sight, when the object is not clearly discerned at what distance soever it be placed.

Doctor Copper finished tearing. He put the pieces in his mouth and looked at Mr Benjamin like a spaniel.

Mr Benjamin was not seeing him.

Grumph, he said, was no expert in codes, nor was Mr Dickens exactly a professional hunter of hidden meanings. But they thought, and I think, that if this bloody letter on my bloody buttocks did not say a whole lot more to bosom friend Smith than it has done to all the bloody investigators who have laughed it off as gibberish without examining the bloody words in it, then . . . then . . . then a good life is the only bloody religion!

He tugged at his black eyepatch, making it twang against his bony eye-socket. There was nothing wrong with the eye underneath.

Smith, he went on blandly, was involved in unnamed scandals the very next year. He had to leave Bristol and only came back when the storm had blown over, to live into lecherous old age, doing odd jobs as doorkeeper at the theatre. (The stage is the best school of morality.) Note the greeting— Infallible Doctor. Grumph did. And he said to himself, and Mr Dickens (Mr Stephens had gone back to his ink), Isn't it likely that William Smith was being invited to read *medical* equivalents into the fantastic words of the letter?

Doctor Copper began swallowing the chewed scraps of paper. They tasted like new false teeth.

If this still seems incredible to your reverence, said Mr Benjamin patiently, let us recapitulate the circumstances. In April Chatterton had threatened suicide after affairs with at least two girls who, if not prostitutes in a London sense, were whores in Bristol fashion. Just before this he had written doggerel about the girls having green sickness. In London he had noted that Carty's trade is dwindled into nothing here—a man may starve by it, but he must have luck indeed, who can live by it. Later, he had sent condolences in the misfortune of Mrs Carty. He says, My advice is leech her temples plentifully, keep her very low in diet, as much in the dark as possible. Nor is this last prescription the whim of an old woman. Whatever hurts the eyes affects the brain, and the particles of light, when the sun is in the summer signs, are highly prejudicial to the eyes, and it is from this sympathetic effect, that the headache is general in summer. But, above all, talk to her but little, and never contradict her in any thing. This may be of service. I hope it will. Now, señor, who the Cartys were, and what Carty's trade was, and what disease Mrs Carty had—I have never seen suggested. But two lines of a prostitute's curse ring in the head as though they belong here:

> pray Excep of me Love Hartley
> an send me word Cartingley.

I am, of course, aware—as Grumph and Mr Dickens were aware—that the symptoms Chatterton talks of are innocent enough to describe what we now call migraine. Yet what if they were but half a reflection of what he felt himself? (You must know I have long been troubled with a poetical Cephalophonia.) The summer lights, Mein Herr, the bloody lights of summer were making the marvellous boy dream of blindness—and then there was a horrid cold he had suddenly gone down with in June. Another letter had talked of a most horrible wheezing in his throat. And this is the very letter

136

that someone (his sister or his mother?) has rendered illegible for some lines at the point where he is to tell how, half-undressed, he caught the cold. I quote: There was a fellow and a girl in one corner, more busy in attending to their own affairs . . . And which continues (after the erased passage) with an obscure reference: The nymph is now an inhabitant of one of Cupid's inns of court. The same letter which says darkly: However, my entertainment, though sweet enough in itself, has a dish of sour sauce served up in it.

Mr Benjamin leaned forward. His glass fell, and smashed. He ignored it.

Your serene highness, he said slowly, there can be little doubt that *Chatterton killed himself because he was convinced he had the Pox!*

He sat back.

Doctor Copper shut his eyes, and gulped.

Whether or not he actually had it, said Mr Benjamin, or merely suffered from headaches, cramps, pains, migraine, night sweats, and a gleet that made him *imagine* he had it, I am not qualified to judge, and doubt if we shall ever know. On the one hand, he would not be the first bloody adolescent to have killed himself for fear that he had contracted venereal disease. On the other, Chatterton must have checked his symptoms thoroughly against the medical textbooks that shit Barrett had given him and the others he had instructed his sister to send on from Bristol. The girl who said, I haive a man an man shall haive me, and whose house was not built with stavis had wished him a good gonery. Grumph thought about that a lot, signor, a lot. His conclusion? Was it not much as one might say, A Merry Syphilis and a Happy Gonorrhoea? It may just as likely have been syphilis as far as I can tell, but there would be justice in it if she was right. I am no crossword-puzzler, mynheer, but if I were I might solve the letter to William Smith as Mr Dickens did. By varying the *feet* of the metrical words in it, as Chatterton seems to invite on one level of its interpretation, one can anagrammatise SYPHILIS, CHATTER-

1*   137

TON, DIAGNOSIS, GONORRHOEA, ARSENIC and SUICIDE from the suspicious phrases. The Rev Michael Lort's puzzled report, Cross says he had the foul disease, is thus seen to be no less than the truth.

He stretched and scratched himself and laughed. One word more, he said. Robert Browning, hearing of Grumph's researches, wrote an essay about the Chatterton case, in which he commented, on this letter reprinted on my buttocks: SMEGMA—*ointment, we suppose.*

He leered knowingly. I shall not quarrel with him for what he supposes, he said, but will merely point out to you, if it pleases your Eternity, what neither Robert bloody Browning nor my grandfather nor Mr twerpy Dickens nor anyone else has ever pointed out. Chatterton was hardly going to spend his last two weeks down here attaining the mystery of composing smegma if smegma was a detergent soap. It is true that both Kersey and Bailey give: SMEGMA: soap or anything that scours. But, as the O.E.D. notices, there is no evidence at all that the word was ever current in English in this sense. It has another meaning that fits the character of the true Chatterton—as opposed to the Chatterton of Wallis's idolatrous portrait. SMEGMA—a sebaceous secretion, especially that found under the prepuce. In other words, the thick cheesy growth found under the foreskin and formed by the glands of the penis!

He hummed miserably to himself, then went on: My point is that Browning knew this meaning as well as anyone else—as well as he knew that the Chatterton case had never been scientifically examined except by my grandfather. Is Sordello Chatterton? Browning? Pah! Browning could write, That there should have been a controversy for 10 minutes about the genuineness of any 10 verses of Rowley is a real disgrace to the scholarship of the age in which such a thing took place. Yet his own scholarship with regard to a letter, not a poem, consists in that silly *ointment, we suppose*! Perhaps you think I'm being hard on Browning? There have been others to prefer the legend to the reality, because the legend is harmless, who prefer to think of the marvellous boy rather than the Chatterton who cracked jokes about curates riding on bishopricks and who wrote that unprintable poem, THE EXHIBITION, occasioned by a case of indecent exposure concerning a Bristol clergyman. Grr!

He clasped his hands behind his head and rubbed his toes together. There is poetic bloody justice, he murmured, in the story of the secret copy of a portrait of Chatterton that was given to Southey. Southey, like Byron, was fond of saying Chatterton was mad. This portrait haunted Southey's rooms until his death, then passed to Wordsworth. Wordsworth thought Chatterton perished in his pride. Wordsworth had it for seven years. Rossetti came to admire it. Rossetti had a love-dream of Chatterton. This was the Thomas C that Southey, Wordsworth and Rossetti needed. Long after, in 1891, a later owner of the portrait, who was neither a poet nor Southey, Wordsworth, or Rossetti, cut away the back of the frame and found his suspicions confirmed: H. S. Parkman, Bristol, 1837! And you know who this later owner was, comrade? I'll give you three bloody guesses. Yes, right—

But Doctor Copper had him by the throat.

It was their first physical contact.

The doctor was filled with such love and peace as he had never dreamed of. He felt a great coherence of calm in looking at Mr Benjamin's leathers, at his one bright bird-eye, at the way his face smiled on one side only. He wanted to give him a gift of himself. For the first time in his life, he wanted to be answerable to another human being for all that he was.

Upstairs, he whispered falteringly, in my bedroom, I have a doll's house. And three dolls which, before you came, I could no longer love. Yet now I love them. I love them with all my heart. Would you . . . would you like to see them?

Mr Benjamin looked away. His face was one slow burn of embarrassed bitterness. Gently he shook himself free of the doctor's restraining hand.

What use to me is love? he said.

He went from the terrace then, pausing only to kick the shards of his microscope into the shrubbery, and across the lawn to where his motorcycle lay on its side.

He kicked the big machine into life and rode away without a salute, without looking back, crouched masterful at the handlebars, like an important insect about its sex.

Doctor Copper stood a moment gazing at his flowers without seeing them. Then, feeling very much alone and empty, he went slowly up the stairs to his bedroom and took the dolls from the doll's house, his babyish hands trembling with excitement. But excitement was not enough. It was no use. He did not want them. He could hardly face them.

The Amber Witch

AFTER AMSTERDAM I sailed perhaps three times more, round the world. Then, one sultry afternoon, the air so warm it seemed to hum—where was it? oh, off the Gold Coast, I daresay, but it doesn't truly signify—I fell to thinking again about Emily Brontë, on account of my dead father's love of some of her poems. I suppose, now I come to work it out for your benefit, that what I was really doing was coming, however obliquely, to think of my father himself, after so many years of loveless silence in my head on that subject. Nothing else would explain the way in which Emily shook my consciousness that hot still unremitting afternoon. Remembered lines from her poems, bits of WUTHERING HEIGHTS, details of her small biography (for she had the gift I have sought to be given: of living smally), all this began to run round and round, scampering in my heart so that I could scarce keep up with myself. Of course, there was no copy of her poems on board ship. I had to fret at my memory for two weeks, until we docked at Tilbury, in England. England! O Sterne, pray for me. O Carroll, play for me. O Munchausen, pay for me. England!

I went boldly to the Gravesend public library and stole Emily's POEMS, so ably edited by C. W. Hatfield. Armed with this, I hired a car and a driver, sat back, and proceeded to Haworth Parsonage.

As my driver, ex-RAF ace, blond, taciturn, with only one arm, his mouth so thin and tight that it looked as if it had been made with a knife after the rest of him was finished, sped me with nonchalant skilfulness through the thoughtful green of the

141

English landscape, I reflected, and not for the first time, on my purpose in life.

I did not wish to eliminate my personality.

No.

But I hoped devoutly that in the process of living I could pursue certain instinctive leanings, such as the desire for warmth, to their conclusion, and that *there* I might find the property of my personality sold, as it were, to someone else, made passive, on a higher level of accordance with myself. I could not expect to pass beyond my glum selfregardingness without pain of a visionary nature. Certain *persons* were responsible for me, physically and metaphysically, and it was up to me to name them and know them, reduce them to order, that I might *arrive at the beginning* of my own supersensual existence.

Yes.

My conscience had been buried at birth. My life was a journey : to find the grave and sow my seed in it.

I had lost touch, I realised, as the car joined the Al, with conscious love. I had hope of consciousness : no more. I did not really inhabit Rufus Coate's and Simple's view of the gradually light-redeemed world, the Christified universe. That did not balance with my experience. I had known too many and too bitter wakings to be satisfied with either night or day. I was a man chased by his own selflove, driven by necessary selfengendered illuminations, hopelessly in search of the selfless tomorrow. I decided that it would be a considerable help if I could summon up all the faces of my enemies, and recognise them.

Now I ate a crystallised violet and went over in my head the few facts that had presented themselves to me, that had *forced* themselves, indeed, on my attention. These were almost enough, I reckoned, for the thing to be considered a 'case'. The details of my life, and the details hanging over 'unsolved' and unresolved from lives anterior to mine, had fallen naturally into place. A pattern emerged, and the pattern was this.

142

Sometime in the eighteen fifties my grandmother, Mary Murder, had been tried for a crime she may or may not have committed. Her victim—*if* she was guilty (and I suspect that Mr Minnow's motive has been overlooked)—had been an innocent young Frenchman from the Channel Islands; in other words, not a 'real' Frenchman but a person like myself, not of the French persuasion yet infected with the Gallic disease. Released on a splendid verdict of *Not Proven*, my grandmother had then married an artist, Wardle, who had brought her into contact with the Pre-Raphaelite gang. She had been known, presumably, to Rossetti and Howell. Now the only woman who had stood, so to speak, between Rossetti and Howell, was the woman of the picture Rossetti had drawn, the unknown woman of great beauty, the beautiful face, delicately drawn, and shaded in pencil, with a background of pure gold, whose identity had obsessed my stepfather, the egregious Count C. According to Treffry Dunn, Howell had torn the portrait out of Rossetti's book in circumstances which were obviously chosen, engineered, waited for, because they gave Rossetti no room to protest... It had been done in public, brazenly, coolly, *because Howell was confident Rossetti would not dare disclose the woman's name.* Was there not more than a strong possibility that the woman of the picture had been Mary Murder? Especially as Rossetti had been fascinated—I almost said, *enthralled*—enough by her, and by her story, to draw the picture whose subject was too dreadful: the picture which hung in his rococo shrine of a bedroom, and which Howell had taken care to have a chance to inspect when Rossetti was absent.

But, then, why had Howell been murdered? Why the half-sovereign clenched between his teeth in that Chelsea gutter where he had been discovered with his throat cut?

Not only *why* . . . but *who* . . . ?

Who killed Howell? And where did the Wandering Jew fit in? And Masterman Simple? And Captain Rufus Coate, with his unconditional hatred of music?

I felt sure that there was some common denominator which, once perceived, grasped, and acted upon, would make clear to me *the plot against my family*—for, yes, already it was plain as day that someone or something, a devilish *person* or *persons* belonging to an organisation of such wickedness that it could easily operate from generation to generation, existed to thwart and destroy our house . . . The curse which held my mother softly spellbound in the priory garden, which had killed my father, and nearly brought my grandmother to the gallows, this was now at work upon me . . .

I fell asleep then, lulled by the warmth and security of the car, my travelling womb. The next thing I knew we were in Haworth. I stepped out and stood for the first time in fact where I had often stood in fiction—at the windy top of that steep grey street flanked by little stone houses, before the church with its blunt tower, the well-populated grave-yard of cool slatecoloured tombstones, the setts, and the parsonage.

I paid off my driver and set about finding lodging for the night. At last settled in a comfortable room of a house not far from the church, I ate a merry supper and then stretched out my hands to the fire and examined in myself the impulse which had sent me hurrying on a strange pilgrimage of passion across half England.

I had been drawn hither by a woman's poems. Not even by all of those, but by one in particular, the three stanzas beginning *There let thy bleeding branch atone*, which my father had been fond of reciting.

Fond of reciting!—Nay. From an early age he had pressed and impressed those verses on me as if they held the key to our family mystery. I took out the Hatfield edition, in its familiar and reassuring green bindings, from my small but bloodstained luggage, and read the poem again.

If I had expected my presence in Haworth to make the poem fly open and admit me to its most secret happenings of meaning, I was disappointed.

144

I smoked a skinny cigar from the small band of them I always carry in my cap, and went to bed.

But I could not have slept more than an hour or so when a handful of gravel was thrown against my window and I leaned my head out to see a gigantic Chinaman standing in the steep street. He was so tall that his dreadful eyes were on a level with my own, although I was a storey up. He was shifting miserably from foot to foot, as if he wanted to urinate, his sweaty pigtail grotesque in the moonlight, a magnificent specimen of its kind, hanging from its owner's back like the pennant from the main truck of a man-of-war. He wore white satin garments with a bright blue button upon his chest. In his right hand he clutched a rolled silk umbrella. On the plaid travelling-rug draped over his left shoulder, sat a dwarf with spider arms.

To cut a long story short, I dressed quickly and the three of us proceeded to Luddenden Foot, at the dwarf's suggestion. The train pulled in there as bleak dawn was breaking; rather, there was no true or new light, only the leavings of moonlight remained about us as we walked by the canal.

You realise, said the Chinaman politely, that this is the place where Branwell went wrong? He kept a notebook here writing *Jesu*! on every page . . . But then you knew that he was in love with Emily?

I thought it better to say nothing. I did indeed remember that it was at this place—Luddenden Foot, I mean—that Branwell Brontë had been posted in his employ on the new Leeds and Manchester Railway (later known as the Lancashire and Yorkshire Railway). In those days Luddenden Foot had been but newly established as a station. Branwell had been occupied here as stationmaster cum clerk.

I looked about me as we paced. Luddenden Foot lay towards the middle of the nineteenth century. It was a derelict, unpleasing place. In truth, it depresses me now in memory so profoundly that I cannot bring myself to describe it.

I sat on one of the Chinaman's shoulders. The dwarf was

on the other. He achieved this position by swinging himself up on his master's pigtail.

Why? I asked the Chinaman; and I was prepared to substantiate the mere bald (or balding) query with the rest of the questioning spirit that was upon me, had he not taken my unattended word as a signal for him to flow into speech, into a speech which—so I fancied—he had prepared long since, and carefully consigned to heart, and (perhaps) already had occasion to deliver to others than myself.

Name, said the Chinaman, of Chang. I am always seventeen summers old. I am a native of Fychow, a city in the Auwhy province of the celestial Chinese empire, latterly tampered with by Levellers, but no matter. I wish to make clear to you the way in which Howell obtained certain chairs belonging to me, chairs which he sold to Dante Gabriel Rossetti. Not only chairs, either. No. More than chairs. But, first, it is my unpleasant duty to explain to you that the poem you so admire—the poem which I believe your honourable father was wont to recite, and which has led to your present location within our company (which we are glad of, and greet you for)— that this poem should properly be read in the context of the Gondal story created by Emily and her sister Anne. Ah, my friend, I see you hide a yawn—or is it a smile?— with your too polite hand . . . I beg you, listen attentively, do not permit yourself the selfdefensive luxury of boredom. You can so ill afford it! We are here, my dwarf Badcock and myself, to advise you how best to destroy what you call your self, which is an incomplete engine grossly overrated by certain philosophers of—but you know all this? Good. Enough of themes. To dark particulars. The Gondal saga may depress you as a subject of small interest, as something of fascination only to Brontë scholars, perhaps you may even have skipped the pages dealing with it, when reading any of the too numerous works which deal with them?

I admitted that it was so.

It would have been well, said Chang, had you stayed to

consider whether that was not precisely the reaction Emily Brontë *wanted* to draw from you, and gone on from that to wonder why she should wish that you would *not* read the matter . . . Yes, I say matter. My friend, within the Gondal story, Emily concealed her—if you will permit a nonbiological truism—heart, even as Shakespeare did, not (as Wordsworth and his disciples have thought) in his sonnets, written in any case by Anne Hathaway, but in his *plays*, the last place anyone would think of looking for it. In Shakespeare's case, which I shall not go into just now, it was a question of money (he loved the esoteric stuff even as Rimbaud did) and therefore of satisfying the public while at the same time communicating certain most unpublic—private in the best sense—truths to an audience which could only have been infinitely small in his own time, and which has hardly been augmented since. In Emily's case, and with a similar wisdom to impart, what better place to hide it than *the parlour*, in the playbox, in a socalled game played with her sister Anne? That Anne was ignorant of the real significance of Gondal is obvious from her contributions to it. But examine Emily's Gondalling and any man who is—shall we say?—sensitive to the mysteries (I think you understand me well enough) becomes inordinately excited. His excitement may seem inexplicable to himself; in his blind casting about, he may even be forced to conclude that it has something to do with the quality of the poems as poetry. Let me assure you that it is not so. Remember your own experience . . . You heard one poem which your father was fond of reciting aloud from memory. In fact that poem is a fragment—I mean it should be considered as a *part* of the whole wisdom won by Emily. Look at it in your mind as a sentence, a communication. One sentence. Now think of it as it should be—within a paragraph. And the paragraph within a chapter. And the chapter within what we might call 'the story'. You begin to see what I am driving at? Emily had certain—shall we say?—'spiritual information' (and I use the term in quotemarks, as shorthand, you appreciate) which she

147

wished both to reveal and conceal, to publish and not publish, to put on record for those who have eyes to see. What should she do with such information? Tell me, have you read E. A. Poe's *The Purloined Letter?*

I admitted that I had.

Then you will understand why she made no attempt to communicate her heart's truth in those novels of hers, said Chang. Instead, she chose the Gondal saga. A cunning and correct decision, when you reflect on the two facts in your own experience of her—first, that you were deeply attracted, drawn into her orbit even to the extent of journeying here, by one of the *deliberate fragments* of her 'system'; second, that you had lazily dodged that 'system' in its worked-out form as the socalled Gondal saga, skipping the pages which tried to come to terms with it in the standard biographies and the orthodox criticisms. My friend, my dear friend, had you read those pages you skipped you might have smelt for yourself—a person of your perception and with such a long nose—that *the commentators know nothing about it*. They are completely in the dark, to a man. Every comment and commentary on the Gondal saga is—as it were—written by Anne Brontë, the innocent unknowing one, taking the view that it is a pleasing romantic fiction, a higher game, a feat or flight or feint of the playful imagination. No one has grasped the mask and seen behind it. No one has understood what Emily meant by Gondal as a whole, though there are those—like yourself—who have been fatally infected by the beauty (the truth, even) of the parts.

He paused. The dwarf handed him a sheet of paper. Chang consulted it briefly.

We have another nine minutes, he said.

And what then, I asked.

Then you must do as you see fit, said Chang. Take the train back to Haworth. Take a car back to your ship. Take a boat back to France. Fugue off to Matraval. Whatever you need.

I said, And you?

Chang smiled. The dwarf he had called Badcock—and where had I heard the name before?—smiled also.

We shall be busy, said Chang. We have to see a man about some horses for the King of Spain.

I let this pass. I said, What you have told me about the Gondal saga interests me very much indeed. Will you not tell me more? Will you give me the key to it? I have the poems here, as you have noticed— (I held up the Hatfield edition and was alarmed when Chang spat)— I would dearly love to know how to read them.

My friend, said Chang, not unkindly, you ask the impossible.

Of course, I said.

If I could answer your request in eight minutes we should neither of us need to be down here, Chang explained.

Very well, I said. What *can* you tell me then?

I can tell you, said Chang, how Howell got my chairs for Rossetti. Wait! Do not begin to look angry in your heart. The anecdote does not put the story out of joint. It is all one.

Go on, I said.

Chang went on : After my first appearance in London, in 1865, a gentleman came to see me in my private rooms. I was averse then—as now—to giving interviews to individual members of that monster which (for the sake of making a life, you understand) I called 'the public'. Also, at that time I did not choose to let it be generally known that I could speak the English tongue, and my reluctance to do so made any immediate discourse a bore—I had to go through the motions of relying on an interpreter, either my dwarf Badcock or my so-called wife, King Foo, the Honest Lily. However, this gentleman was both obstinate and determined. He climbed in through the window in an opera cloak and offered me six pornographic books (very tedious sadistic stuff, all high heels and complicated corsets and thin birch rods, not at all to my fantastic taste), and a portrait of the poisoner Mary Murder for my—

Wait a bit, I cried. Are you sure it was Mary Murder?

Of course, said Chang.

How? I asked.

Chang smiled. It would take more than a shilling's worth of arsenic to kill me, he said. I assure you that the picture was of Mary Murder and no other. The gentleman gave it to me in exchange for two chairs belonging to me, some bronze statuary, and a pint of my blood.

What did he want with your blood? I demanded. It *was* Howell, wasn't it?

The answer to your second question is a partial yes, said Chang. The answer to your first question is that Mary was thirsty.

I let this pass. I said, What was Howell like?

A Portuguese Jew, said Chang. Elegant and plausible. Lean. Hawkfaced. Hook nose. Dark bushy sidewhiskers accentuating the pallor of his skin. I should say shortsighted, but far too vain to wear spectacles.

Did he tell you he had a weak heart? I asked.

Chang frowned. I think not, he said.

Were his shoes rather lovingly polished? I asked.

He wore no shoes, said Chang.

This was disturbing. I had no time, however, to reflect on it immediately, for Chang and the dwarf Badcock on his shoulder were making ready to quit my company. The parting was a very formal affair. I won't go into it. I will set down here only the one important fact, that as we shook hands across Chang's throat the dwarf took the opportunity to slip something into my palm. When they had climbed into the down train and Chang had folded himself up and they were gone, I looked at my hand and saw what the dwarf had pressed upon me. It was the sort of band that is commonly used for holding a table napkin. It had a design upon it. The design was of a snake swallowing its own tail, making a perfect circle.

I had not seen such a thing, ever, in my life, but I remembered that my father had sometimes spoken of a ring like this in The Game. I put it in my cap and determined to study it at my leisure. Also I resolved that I would question the dwarf Badcock closely on the subject of my father, should we chance to meet again.

I took the next train back to Haworth. An idle enquiry of the ticket collector told me that Chang and his companion had not alighted here. Thinking over the blue button he had worn I had begun to wonder, however, if the 'Chang' I had met might not have been an impostor—not Chang, but his brother, Chang Sou Gow, 'the Public Diamond'. How tall had the real Chang been? I could not remember rightly; but surely too tall to enter a railway compartment, even though doubled up?

I went to my lodging and paid my bill, saying urgent business demanded that I break short my vacation. Why I bothered to make these excuses, I know not. Put it down to my temperament—which has always been shy and retiring, snail-like, nervy, timorous. I am, in so many respects where I should be a man, a jellyfish.

I went then and stood in Haworth churchyard and watched the children skipping from tombstone to tombstone.

What Chang, or Chang Sou Gow, had told me of the Gondal saga, made me excited. I mean, it excited me. Yes. I noticed that my hands were shaking as I lit a cigar. I do not usually notice such things. If there was spiritual nourishment for the taking in those Gondal poems then I would eat and drink of them. I needed such provender in my quest. Also I had more than a suspicion that a proper, a *total*, reading of the poems might well prove relevant to my understanding of the puzzle I moved in, the maze I was seeking to get to the centre of, the mystery that beset me on every side.

I was aware that the greatest living authority on the Brontës —Miss Rosetta Eponym—had a house in Essex. I went into the Brontë museum (a thing I would not otherwise have dreamed of doing, on account of the wallpaper) to find out the name of the village, which I remembered having seen appended to the introduction of more than one of her books on the subject. Yes, the name of the village was Wethersfield.

Despite what Chang Sou Gow had said about the Brontë scholars knowing nothing of the esoteric significance or meaning of Gondal, I had developed the idea that this woman could help me. I clung to that idea, hired a car, and this time drove myself south again.

Wethersfield was one of those villages which seem not only to be asleep, but in process of being dreamed by someone somewhere else.

I enquired at the public house. No one had heard of Miss Rosetta Eponym.

She is, I said condescendingly, the greatest living authority on the Brontës.

No one had heard of the Brontës. I noticed that there was a picture by Burne-Jones over the fireplace. Appropriate, I thought.

A writer, I suggested.

Just then there occurred a considerable commotion in the crowded saloon bar where I was standing. Have I said that it was a frosty stiffbacked January evening, just before closing time according to English licensing laws and Essex habits? Well, that is how it was. And consequently there was a splendid logfire burning in the grate, where bizzare locals in boots and jeans and pointed shoes stood together to toast their buttocks.

And, at that moment, as I mentioned that Miss Rosetta Eponym was a writer, a thrush fell down the chimney and caught fire in the grate and flapped out, its wild wings frantic and blazing, and flew round the room with piteous music.

The sight horrified me—not least because I recognised some sinister hand again at work in the disposition of my destiny,

152

for had not my father within the context of The Game, impressed upon my tender mind a memory of his own childhood, just like this, of a thrush that fell down the chimney and flew about the room, its wings ablaze?

As if that were not enough to melt my spine, the boots and jeans and pointed shoes instantly adopted what I can only 'describe' as a very strange attitude indeed, towards the burning bird. No sooner had it flown free and terrible with flames into the bar than they began stamping and shouting rhythmically, as if conducting some barbarous fertility rite in which the firebird figured. The words of their chant were hard to make out. Was it my own fevered imagination, caught by the sudden hostility I felt in the scene—a hostility which turned itself against me as an intruder, a witness to sights I could not understand or participate in—was it this that made me hear the words as: Howell! Howell! Howell!?[1]

The thrush fell dead at my feet in a charred ball.

Everyone suddenly burst out laughing.

With blind eyes, I turned for the door. I had taken only a few steps, dazed by darkness, across the frosty green and back towards my car where it stood in a patch of moonlight, when a hand plucked at my sleeve.

Yer wanna see Rosy? said a voice.

It was a child, a small girl, perhaps twelve years old. She was not a nymphet. I know that in looking at her my mind was on something else—I was remembering that Chang (or his brother) had referred to his companion, the dwarf, in Luddenden Foot, as Badcock, and I had accepted this, whereas the Chang whose chairs had ended up in Rossetti's bedroom near the Bryant and May's matchbox and the symbolic picture of my mother's mother, Mary Murder, *this* Chang had had a dwarf called Chung Mow, who had looked like Humpty Dumpty, a dwarf who had a trick of bending his right hand

[1] It has been suggested to me that, allowing for Essex pronunciation, the chant may have been a Learish *Howl, howl, howl*! However, I doubt it. My own interpretation fits the facts.

153

at quick angles to the wrist. Were Badcock and Chung Mow the same? I doubted it. If they were not—did it not mean that Chang was not Chang either, that he might be Chang Sou Gow, or Chung-li Chuan, first of the Eight Immortals, whose symbol is a heartshaped fan, or even another Chinese monstrosity? These were pertinent questions.

Yer wanna see er or not, mister?

The child was patient. I said I did indeed want to see Rosy, if Rosy was Miss Rosetta Eponym, the eminent Brontë scholar.

The Bronts, said the child knowingly. Yeh. Thass er.

How she had known I wanted Miss Eponym I cannot pretend to guess. I hardly think that she was present in that jovial company in the public house, though of course she may have been there concealed among the gaitered legs. In any case, she led me now through deep lanes and across turnipped fields in the moonlight until we came to a hut and, without knocking, entered.

E was askin fer yer, the child said prettily, and left.

The only light in the hut was from a long candle burning in a boat on the table. By its jostling illumination I made out a bed in the corner. It was a big bed, brassy and ornate, that looked as though it had seen years of service in a Victorian brothel. An old woman lay on it under a pile of fur coats. A cat was sitting on her chest. It was hard to tell which was cat and which was fur coats. The woman's face was blue. She spoke with difficulty. Obviously, she was dying.

Without more ado I handed her the only credential—indeed, the only clue—I had: the snake-ring given to me by the dwarf Badcock.

She looked at it and giggled briefly.

Mary send you then? she said.

Mary? I said. No. Chang.

Chang? she said. Who in the name of shit is Chang?

I said, It is not important, madame. But, tell me, this Mary . . . My mother's mother—

154

Little royner, she said, I'm old enough to be your grand-mother. So you just shut your gob and listen to me.

I did so.

As I set about listening I noticed that the candle was arranged somewhat cunningly in its boat. A loop of thread ran from the base of it to the waiting wick of the next candle, ready in another boat, identical with the first, a few inches off. And from the foot of this candle another piece of thread, et cetera. Thus, Miss Eponym could have light all night without needing to get out of bed.

I see you are admiring my fairy lamplighter, said she.

Most ingenious, madame, I murmured.

Severn's idea, she said.

I beg your pardon, I said, I don't think I know—

Severn, she said, Severn. The big gelding who went out to Rome with John Keats.

Oh, yes, I said.

Miss Eponym smiled with weary cynicism. At any rate, she said, it's a comfort to think that I'll soon be lying in Beelze-bub's bosom.

I corrected her: Surely you mean Abraham's?

Huh, said Miss Eponym, if you'd been a widow as long as I have then you wouldn't care what the name was that went with it.

Her blue eyes looked gravely at me a while without seeing. She took a pinch of snuff, first at one nostril, then at the other. Her only energy seemed inspired by anger. Little coistrell, she said, I don't know you from damned Adam, and I don't know anyone who does, but I'm going to trust you because you bear dear bloody Mary's ring and also because, let us admit it, I am dying, and no one else is likely to turn up here out of the dark this last night of my life, eh?

She broke into a terrible spasm of wet coughing. I was of what assistance I could be. She seemed grateful. When it had passed she lay back in the pillows and stroked the cat with a hand that was unnervingly fat and flabby in the candlelight.

155

I noticed that her eyes had changed colour. They were now brown.

Little groffe, she said at last, I want you to rip open my combinations. Come, come, you freckled fool, don't blush. They are there, on the chair. You'll find something in the gusset. Don't waste time. I've pissed my last piss. *I haven't all night.*

Madame, I said, it pleases me to find one so witty and resourceful at the approach of death, but—

Cut the caties and rip the knickers, she ordered. Put your finger in the hole. That's it. Good. Grand. Lovely. Now—rip!

I did so. A thick tattered black notebook and a yellow piece of newspaper fell to the floor. I bent to retrieve them.

The newspaper was a cutting from the *Times* of November the eleventh, 1865.

Read it, said Miss Eponym.

I read, as follows:

THE SKULL OF BEN JONSON

In the course of a paper read this week by Dr Kelburne King, president of the Hull Literary and Philosophical Society, before the members of that Society, on The Recent Visit of the British Association to Birmingham, the Doctor, in speaking of a visit which he and Dr Richardson, of London, had made to Shakespeare's birthplace, at Stratford-on-Avon, narrated the following curious incident: He said that a blind gentleman, who thought no one but the guide was present, mentioned that a friend of his had a relic which would be a valuable addition to the Shakespearean Museum at that place—the skull of Ben Jonson, When this friend attended the funeral of Dr C—, at Westminster Abbey, he perceived that the next grave, that of Ben Jonson, had been opened, and he could see the skeleton of the body in the coffin. He could not resist the opportunity of putting in his hand

156

and extracting the skull, which he placed under his cloak and carried off. From a remark which the blind gentleman dropped, Dr Richardson thought he could identify the offender, and he asked if the person was not reputed to be a Portuguese, and if his initials did not consist of certain letters. The blind gentleman was not a little startled at finding that his secret was out; he admitted the fact, but prayed that no advantage might be taken of the discovery. This was promised; but as Dr Richardson is an ardent admirer of the Avonian Bard, he is determined that, without going to extremities, he will bring the necessary pressure to bear on the possessor of the skull, so that it shall be placed in a more worthy repository than the cabinet of an obscure individual.

Miss Eponym said, I will allow you one guess as to the initials.

C.A.H.? I suggested.

You catch on quickish, said Mrs Eponym. There's some as have thought you blind.

Your statement, madame, I said, suggests that you know more of me than you have led me to suppose.

Never mind what I know or don't know, said Miss Eponym. You can't skeat your way out of this. I want you to keep that cutting. I want you to promise me you will not rest until it is safely in the hands of Her Majesty.

Her Majesty? I said. The Queen?

How many other Her Majesties do you know? she demanded. Really, they put some funny bowkies on the way these days.

Miss Eponym, I said politely, I came to you because you are acknowledged to be the leading English authority on the Brontës.

Oh, she said, those.

Yes, I said.

What about em? she said.

I wanted to ask you, I said, what you thought of the Gondal business.

Thought? said Miss Eponym.

Think, I said.

What *I* think of it? Miss Eponym persisted, or what I've heard others think of it?

I said: Both, really, I suppose. Your final opinion of Gondal, in fact.

The old woman cackled. This brought on another bout of coughing that left her anhelous, more than ever shrunken into the dirty pillows, her pinched face like a monk's, her eyes now green.

Yes, she said, it's likely to be my final opinion. Quick, now, little faitour. What do you want to know about Gondal? Why bother your pretty head with such stuff?

I hesitated. The giant Chang Sou Gow, I said, told me that—

I don't want to hear feerie fairy stories on my last night down here, Miss Eponym broke in irritably.

I apologise, I said. I read Emily's poem which begins *There let thy bleeding branch atone*, and began to think about her.

Better, said Miss Eponym. Distinctly bloody better. Yes. A feetyve fair sort of start, in fact. Now Miss Ratchford places that poem in section seven of her arrangement of the poems into an epic of Gondal—in that section of poems unplaced in the story pattern, and grouped together under the general heading, Poems of memory and remorse. Just think what Emily Jane would've said to that! It was probably written when she was about twentytwo.

Yes, I said, but Gondal?

Gondal, said Miss Eponym, was the perfect country.

I was surprised to hear her give such a definitive opinion. In what sense? I asked.

In the only sense that makes sense, she said.

158

The perfect country? I repeated.

The country, said Miss Eponym, that Simple was smething around for at the ends of the earth, and others have found by staying at home. That other Emily, for a start.

Other? I queried.

Yes, said Miss Eponym, what's her name . . . ? Wore white. Something about a reticent volcano and presentiment is that long shadow on the—

Ah, I said, Dickinson.

If you like, said she.

I considered a moment, then decided to refuse this alternative. I wanted to get back to what I took to be the subject. I said, But I understood Simple to have been a missionary.

Little crevent, said Miss Eponym kindly, this is a complicated world, where lovers live by love as larks by leeks. You are yourself confused by yourself.

I admitted that this was so.

One thing you have clear, she went on, eyes black and shining in a new face of sternness turned towards me. Your promise. You have understood it?

Not to rest, I said, until this cutting from your knickers is in the hands of the Queen.

Good boy, she said. I like your moral fibre. Now I think it's high time you had a cup of cocoa.

She pointed out to me where the tin was. I made two cups, but I noticed she hardly touched hers—and when I offered to hold the cup to her lips she said she was beyond accepting such gallantry.

I observed her looking at me closely.

Laddie, said she, are you strong?

Not particularly, I admitted. I am a martyr to Our Lady Insomnia. Also I suffer from debilitating colds.

She giggled. They'll do ye noo harm, she said.

It was odd, yet I could have sworn that her voice was taking on a sudden and disconcerting *Scots* accent. And why did this

159

seem to me sinister, there in the candlelight in the hut on the outskirts of Wethersfield? I, who had no reason to fear the Scot . . .

Drink it up, laddie, urged Miss Eponym.

I have, I said.

Another wee drappie? she said.

No, thanks, I said. I was hoping you might be able to tell me a little more about Gondal.

Faugh, said Miss Eponym, you smell of the Glasgow underground!

If you don't mind, I said. You see, madame, I came from Chang Sou Gow and Badcock—

Who? she demanded.

Chang Sou Gow, I said.

Fegs, she said.

I beg your pardon, I said.

No him, said Miss Eponym. The other bastard.

Badcock, I said.

Fegs, said Miss Eponym.

What? I said.

No, said Miss Eponym.

What? I said.

No *Badcock*, said Miss Eponym.

I stumbled to my feet. By God, madame, I shouted, by God, by God, you are right! His name is—his name is—

And, at this point—(I am ashamed to admit)—I passed out there across Miss Rosetta Eponym's bed, and everything, as Spinoza used to say, became a blank . . . I remember, as I fell, having the feeling that *I* was dying—of some sort of fit or ecstasy—and that the old lady, who would never die, was watching me with sweet amusement, stroking her cat up the wrong way with flabby fingers, her eyes all colours and no colour, her neck goitrous, her lips as red as sealingwax, her hair spread out in the leaping candlelight, glowing and golden and growing, growing, growing, undimmed, at a disgusting rate, writhing about my head, strangling me, throttling me, writing about the room, twisting about the night itself, like a singing nest of golden snakes.

When I came to myself I was in a first class compartment of a railway train. It was night and the country outside was impossible to discern in the rank darkness. I was alone. Beside me on the prickly upholstery of the seat was a yellowed human skull, of some considerable antiquity, very cold and bald and smooth to the touch.

I looked at my reflection in the window of the train—this being an unfortunate habit of mine, for which I humbly beg your wise indulgence—and was little surprised to see that I had put on weight. At a rough reckoning, I estimated that I had gained about six or seven pounds since leaving my ship at Tilbury. The last time I had gained weight at such an obscene velocity was after my father's funeral, when I vowed to give up the secret service for a month, and did so (with two exceptions, which were hardly my fault).

Taking my silver calimeters from the lining of my cap I set about measuring and otherwise scrutinising the skull which was to be my sole companion on earth until the train (a night express, I guessed from the furious hunger with which it was eating up the dark leagues) came to its next stop.

The forehead of the skull was highly polished, classically shaped, the eye-orbits being profound. The teeth had long gone bad. The cheekbones were massive, the jaws powerful but by no means brutish. The skull measured ten inches from top to bottom, five inches from side to side. It was very dry and undoubtedly contractile. I found it hard to gauge exactly how old it might be. Two hundred years, or three . . .

I went through my pockets to see if I had gained or lost anything else (besides the skull and the six pounds of flesh, that is). I discovered that my copy of THE COMPLETE POEMS OF EMILY JANE BRONTË was missing. I was not unduly pleased to find that Miss Rosetta Eponym's cutting about Ben Jonson was still in my vest pocket, because I could not for the life of me see how I was ever going to be in a position where I might consign it to the hands of the Queen as I had rashly promised.

There was something else in my pocket.

The little black notebook. It was thick and battered and tattered. From its limp shape it was obvious that pages had been torn out at random, sometime perhaps when some person was short of matches for his pipe. I had forgotten all about it, fascinated with the cutting. But might this not have been the *real* treasure in the old lady's keeping? It would have been like her, plain bloodyminded as she was, to direct my attention to the cutting, so that I came at the truth obliquely, round and about . . .

I opened the little black book.

It was thickpacked with writing in a minute cramped hand, wonderfully legible, but tiny. Like the writing of a changeling. Where had I seen that hand before?

Of course! In the frontispiece to the Hatfield edition! This was a notebook that had belonged to Emily Jane Brontë.

I felt quite faint with excitement, believe me, gentle reader.

I was sure I stood trembling on the verge of some tremendous revelation, of the secret I had sought in so many guises and places.

I flicked through the book impatiently, in a fever of anxiousness.

Yes, as I feared—huge chunks missing. But enough left to make it obvious what the book was. Yes.

I held in my hands the lost manuscript of a novel by Emily Brontë!

I began reading it, lingering over each word to make sure that I had read it correctly. I soon grew accustomed to the handwriting, and then read at my ease.

The book was a fantasy—a wild, strange, poetic work. In some respects it was autobiographical, but only in the distant

162

untouchable way one would expect, giving the whole a fierce yet tender tone, at once personal and removed from 'real' life. Its plot, briefly summarised, so far as I can remember and so far as I could make sense of it what with all the missing parts, concerned a clergyman whose daughter is accused of being a witch. But before witchcraft is shouted in her face, she has made her father rich and stupidly satisfied by bringing him amber from a cave she has discovered on a bleak shore. The girl *is* a witch, and the cave—this is subtly suggested—does not exist. It is her own heart she feeds her father from. She tears out more and more of herself to feed to him, bringing it to him (he is a cold, blunt, insensitive man) as the amber he can sell to finance weird religious schemes of his own devising. When the girl is accused of witchcraft, the priest cannot see the irony of the situation. He devotes himself to her defence, and she is eventually acquitted (but not before sentence has all but been carried out to kill her). He goes back to his blind religiosity, but the girl—in a scene which far surpasses anything in WUTHERING HEIGHTS—goes up to her own funeral pyre on the moorland, and when he comes after her and asks what she is doing, she answers simply, Father, I am burning my heart.

As regards style and treatment, the novel was plainly inferior to WUTHERING HEIGHTS. The touch was not sure; there was fumbling in the handling of the dialogue; the girl, Maris, was wonderfully realised, but the father remained so locked in his doltishness that it was difficult to avoid thinking that the author's lack of sympathy with him was a serious artistic flaw.

All the same, some of the writing was delightful. I remember the first paragraph by heart:

> Trunks and drawers and cupboards and chests and coffers and cases—The heart of the house plucked out, dragged down, broken open, ravished—My surplice itself torn to rags and used disgustingly by some Devil's spawn with

163

thick red hair on the backs of his butcher hands—Oh, oh, oh, but my soul was starting out at my cheeks, yet I smiled and smiled—And they did not find my daughter. At darkfall I had hidden her in the furthest stable among the animals. If I had not taken thought to do so my heart by now had hung in half the heavier, that I am sure of. These black scabby ones wanted already to begin rut with my maid Gretch, a hunchback near fifty winters old—would have done so too, had she not babbled desperate merrily of her weakness of leaking in the act of darkness—I thank my Maker those wild guests are gone, devil-snatched-back, fled away into the same storm that hawked them down on us, their very horses shivering for fright when they put bloody boots across their backs— thank Him that I have at least saved my child from their clutch, although not a speck of flour, nor the meanest grain of corn, not a bit of meat the length of a finger is left, and I know not how I may be powered to keep myself or my Maris from starving—Yet was she safe there among the animals, curled asleep among the warm and breathing animals, and dreamt no harm even as they tore open her dolls and her puppets. She was safekept and I give thanks for that.

The father, the priest, was the narrator, it will be seen. Herein, I suppose, if I was a literary critic, I should say the book's main failure lay. Emily hated this man. She detested his mean, cramped, coarse, blind attitude to his daughter, and skilfully insinuated that there was lechery at the root of it. All the stranger, therefore, that she gave him some of the characteristics of her own father, the Rev Patrick Brontë; on one occasion, for instance, he is shown as bursting into a belltower and setting about the bellringers with his shillelagh, on another he discharges his pistol in the direction of his own church directly across the graveyard on the grounds that, If I hit anyone they're more likely to be already dead—both things

164

the Brontë father is known to have done, the former in his first curacy, at Wethersfield, in Essex, the latter, every morning, at Haworth, from his bedroom window.

All the author's feeling was lavished on the girl, Maris, who therefore ran through the story like a flame.

The poor priest, on the other hand, remained a stone.

But enough! I am not a critic. No. I delighted in the book.

Here is another short passage I remember. Maris is telling her father of a dream, which he, of course, cannot understand:

> Maris said, I dreamed a dream. It was about a woman that ate a worm in her hunger, only the worm burned and became a child within her, only no child but a devil's spectre; and I saw the devil's spectre curled in her womb like a caterpillar on a leaf, and as I saw all this the woman beckoned to me and kissed me when I came to her, only the kiss was cruel and made the blood spurt forth from my finger-ends.

When Maris finds the amber—that is, the outer aspect of her sacrifice for her father's sake—there occurred another memorable paragraph:

> She had been searching for berries in a deep defile near the sea, when her eyes were suddenly dazzled by a brightness down on the shore. She shielded her eyes to look, and saw that it was coming from a cave, dark but for where the sun fell across it, sending an edge of light within. Whichever way Maris walked, this brightness seemed to beckon to her. Intrigued, she gave up worry about the berries and went down the defile to where the brightness was. She found that the wind from the sea had driven off the sand from a vein of amber just inside the cave's mouth. Kneeling in the sand she broke off a

piece of the amber with a stick. She scooped away more sand. She probed. Amber rattled about under the stick wherever she plunged it in. She was surprised by pain in her breast, but broke off more pieces excitedly; then scooped with her hands blindly and found first the one skullsize piece, then the other. She walked a few paces deeper into the cave and then tried again. More amber. She could not thrust her stick in deeper than a hand's depth, and there was amber there, all around. Then she heaped the open place over with sand, and afterward winnowed it with her apron, so that no sign remained. For the rest, no stranger would lightly or likely come thither, seeing that there were no brambleberries about, and she herself had gone that way down the defile more out of wondering, and to look over the sun on the sea, than out of any need. But on the other hand Maris had no fear of not being able to find the cave again. She had marked its threshold with three small white stones, before gathering up the broken amber in her apron and hurrying home.

At home, the priest is allowed one brief moment where he rejoices in the beauty of the amber she has cut for him, as it were, out of her own veins; but he soon begins to think of the profit to be got from it :

> I rubbed the amber with my fingertips—then took up one of the skullsize pieces and held it to my cheek. It was most beautifully cold. Light shone deep in it, so that it seemed I looked through a coloured hole into another world;—perhaps, a world from whence colour came to this.
>
> Washed from the sea, said I.
>
> Maris was playing with two of the smaller pieces, rolling them in her long palm. She said, Washed from the sea, fallen from the heads of dragons or the jaws of a

serpent, bubbled out of the world's thick inner darkness, tumbled headlong out of the autumn sky . . . What does it matter? There is amber there. So much that one might never dream of it all in a single night.

A cave full of amber! said I.

The cave that holds the elusive treasure, said Maris. Look on it, father, and be glad!

I did look on it—and my heart leapt within me. There was dawn in the amber; and autumn darkfall. There was blood in it, and fire, and rust, and wine. Held one way to the light it was flushed, hectic, a fever stone. Held another way, in shadow, the hands cupped round it, it was closer the colour of copper. It was like a wound in the natural order of things. It was vital and spilt itself. It was sacrifice. It was treasure.

I said: It is like the sun itself.

Maris nodded, pleased. Yes, she said, the sun, the whole sun, come forth from its night crossing beneath the sea—the sun dug out as treasure from a cave.

She paused a moment, stroking the smooth top of one of the skullsize pieces, then added, more to herself than myself: The eye would not see the sun if it was not a sun itself.

My child, I said, so soon has God lifted us from our bleak distress, for with this knowledge of amber we shall never need want again.

This knowledge of amber . . . *Knowledge* is exactly what the father lacks, of course; and he *needs* want, cripplingly.

A little later, Maris tells of another dream:

She was walking by the sea when she saw a young man in a coat of red silk and a cloak of scarlet lined with ermine who came riding towards her along the strand. He rode on a high white horse. But the horse bled from a terrible wound between its eyes, and the red drops ran

167

down and fell on the sand, where they were pieces of amber. The young man had on his head a red hat with a white peacock's feather in it. In his hand he held a golden cup. His skin was white and his hair was red— as red as the blood on the nettles, Maris said. He stopped the white horse by my daughter and called her to him, and when she came he leaned down and kissed her on her lips and afterwards offered her to drink from the golden cup. Yet the cup was full of blood and Maris would not drink. Then the young man's white cheeks flushed scarlet as his cloak and he dashed the cup into the foam where, spilling, the blood was again amber. He took from round about his neck a golden chain and before Maris took thought to run away he looped the chain quickly about her, so that she was close bound his prisoner. Then he swung the white horse about and rode into the sea, but the horse was weak with loss of blood, and fell, and the young man was toppled into the water, and as he touched the water—Maris said—he was no more a man but a great bulk of mansize amber, floating in the water, and with a sword thrust into it up to the black hilt. And Maris woke with words on her lips, Wherefore art thou red in thine apparel?—the which I told her were from the prophet Isaiah.

When my daughter had told me this dream I thought long on its meaning. Peradventure the young man figured forth Our Lord, who gave his blood that we might drink of eternal life. But the amber I could not determine.

The poor man never does determine the amber. He is blind to his daughter's suffering (so strangely a parallel, I imagine, to Emily's suffering as a poet in her father's house). He asks her to show him the cave where she found the amber :

At first she was loath. She said, Would you see the blood beating in my heart?

168

I said I did not understand her. Might we not go to the cave and take more amber up from the sand, that we might fetch the more money for it?

Maris sighed. She said, If I do not show you, you will burn for ever. If I do show you, I shall burn for ever. Which do you want?

I laughed at her strange humours. I said, By all means let us go after more amber to the cave, and burn together in the gentle hot of heaven, so it be God's will.

It is, of course, possible that I am missing the whole point of the book's symbolism. A moment ago it crossed my mind that the amber might, in some sense, represent Emily's poems, or the wisdom she spoke out of in her poems. The one thing I am sure of is that it does not just mean amber. The point is, if anything, laboured over, in stressing the father's stupidity in thinking that it is 'just' amber.

Not all the book is concerned with the amber, either. One of the finest supplementary passages is about a ghost:

Several months ago—it seems—a fellow had been racked on the wheel there because he had been tempted by that wicked Satan to slay a wandering handicrafts-man. He died soon enough, but death was not the end of it. Some days after his dying, a carriage passing the gallows where he yet hung on the wheel (which gallows stands on the way through the forest coming back towards us) the racked fellow suddenly moved in the moonlight and sprang down in his black deathsmock onto the back of the carriage, seating himself without a word behind the riding people. The driver whipped up the horses, driving on over the bridge that stands there by the mill. What more happened none knows. The morrow morning a forester found the carriage overturned on the bridge, the horses spiked, the travellers with their throats slit, and one dead of fright with his own hand like a claw at his throat, a half-sovereign between his teeth. Only the driver was alive. He had been thrown from the carriage in its fall, and gone into the millpond. He had made effort to save himself from drowning and reached the bank just before fainting from loss of blood where he had gashed open his head in falling down the bridge. The man had indeed been lucky not to fall into the millwheel. He could tell no more of what had happened than I have told. The magistrates took thought and caused the murderer's body to be taken down from the wheel. They had it buried under the gallows, in hope his ghost would rest. But still it was said he came to sit on the bloody wheel at night time, deathwhite as before, so never man would henceforth go that way.

But the young Alcona, coming through the forest at the time of the fair, and wishing to return straight home with his carriage, did not pause to go the haunted way. I had myself seen him earlier at the inn, and begged him, on account of the ghost, to tarry the night, and go with me on the morrow. But he is an impatient fellow, with a beard like a little spade, and fears neither man nor Devil, and he refused.

Now it was a shrill night and as Alcona came riding along the way he saw the ghost sitting upon the wheel and hardly had he passed by the gallows when the ghost sprang down and set after him. The driver's hair stood up for fright. He whipped his horses on, which had become wild and shy, and shat themselves. The carriage began to ride furiously with a great echo over the bridge that's by the mill. But Alcona, as I've said, lacks some part in him of fear, and turned to look steadfastly over his shoulder at the ghost. Then he marked by the moonlight that in his chase the ghost had trodden flat upon a ball of horsedung.

He thought, This is no ghost!

He shouted to his driver to halt—but the driver chose

not to hear him for the wind. So he sprang from the carriage onto the bridge—no easy feat—unsheathed his thrusting sword, and ran back towards the ghost. When the ghost saw him coming he turned, but Alcona was too quick for him. He smote him with his fist in the neck. The ghost fell to the ground and began wailing.

Young Alcona called his coachman back, where the carriage stood at the far end of the bridge, the horses steaming and shivering in the moon,—and together they bore up the ghost and dragged him back into town, where he was soon named as one Speght, a chandler.

I myself jumped out of bed hearing a noise of shouting in the street and torchlight reaching up through my window to put faces on the walls, and dressed quickly, and ran with the rest in a great throng to see the fellow. He quaked like an aspen leaf, and when he was sharply exhorted—that he would of his own will confess, to save his neck if he'd done no murder—he said that he had had a deathsmock made for him by his wife, dressed himself in it this night, and seated himself on the gallows, in hope of doing some robbery. He had determined to jump into any carriage that passed under, as he had heard the ghost did, and so frighten the travellers that he should easily have their money.

But the young Alcona's carriage had gone too wildly for him to come to grips with it.

Asked had he not been there before and overturned the earlier carriage and slit the throats of those who rode in it, he said: No, that was the ghost! He believed the ghost had been but he had not feared it since he had heard the racked fellow had been put in the ground.

All this, swore the chandler, was truth and nothing but the truth, and he himself had never taken anything from anyone, nor murdered anyone. He prayed that they would forgive him, seeing as he was quite without guilt in the matter of the murder, and whatever had happened

171

when the ghost was abroad in the night was not of his doing.

Ah, but innocent ghost, your innocency was somewhat Devil-patched! The chandler's tale was not wellbelieved; though there were some to wonder publicly how one man could have overpowered the travellers in the coach that had been broken on the bridge, and how a counterfeit could have caused the one to die of terror. Yet the young Alcona laughed at me when I repeated such doubtfulness to him and said had he not proved for once and all that there was no such thing as a ghost?

As for the chandler, he was in turn put to the rack, and given the chance to wear in earnest the black death-smock his wife had stitched for him. Yet it must be said that to the end he protested his innocence.

Well, I think that is enough for it to be seen that although this was in some respects (notably, in the obscure depth of its disturbingness) a book as good as anything Emily ever wrote, she did right not to publish it.

In any case, I learned later that a fortuitous strange event prevented her from doing so—when, in 1841, a German clergyman called Wilhelm Meinhold began publishing what he claimed were the papers of a pastor of Coserow, in Usedom, but which was later to be acknowledged as a romantic novel invention of his own. This work, entitled BERNSTEINHEXE, paralleled Emily's manuscript in certain respects. In each, there was a clergyman who had a daughter. In each, the daughter fetches amber for her father. In each, the family suffers privation through famine. In each, the girl is accused of witchcraft.

There are also similarities odder to explain. The story of Alcona and the ghost is echoed in Meinhold's book, where Alcona has become someone called the Younker of Neinkerken. There are even uncanny resemblances in phraseology and (eccentric) punctuation. But, beyond that, the books are

172

poles apart. Where Emily had genius, Meinhold had nothing. This Younker mentioned soon turns his story into a conventional piece of pretty romance; the girl marries him at the end, after *he* has rescued her most vulgarly from burning. In Emily's manuscript, the girl *wanted* to die, and at the end goes of her own will to her funeral pyre. Also, in Meinhold there is an absence of any real supernatural implications (apart from a colourful old witch who is more comic than anything else)— which is a serious flaw, considering his pastor, Abraham Schweidler, is supposed to be superstitious.

However, it is obviously one of those rare cases where the inferior work, simply by existing, destroys the major one. Emily must have heard something of Meinhold's book, and discovered its similarities to her own. I doubt if she was surprised to learn that such things can happen. There are sometimes dreams that more than one person can dream. Meinhold had shared her dream, and cheapened it, and got first into print. Whether or not she realised that it was only superficially that their novels resembled each other, and whether or not she cared that her own was inestimably greater than his, her strict artistic conscience led her to put her manuscript away and forget about it, I suppose.

The perfect had been ruined by the imperfect.

Later, she wrote WUTHERING HEIGHTS.

That, for what it is worth, is my interpretation of the fact of the book's never having been offered for publication.

I should add—though it barely needs saying—that Meinhold's BERNSTEINHEXE has none of the symbolism I noted as the chief characteristic of Emily's lost novel. In his story, the amber is amber, and that's that. The daughter, in his book, is called Maria. The distance between Maria and Maris is the difference of genius.